# Rowan's Mill

## Elizabeth Walker

KNIGHT

Copyright © 1988 Elizabeth Walker

First published in 1988
by Judy Piatkus (Publishers) Ltd

First published in paperback in 1989
by HEALINE BOOK PUBLISHING PLC

This edition published 2003 by Knight
an imprint of The Caxton Publishing Group

10 9 8 7 6 5 4 3

ISBN 1 84067 2684

Printed and bound in Great Britain by
Cox & Wyman Ltd, Reading, Berkshire

Caxton Publishing Group
20 Bloomsbury Street
London WC1B 3QA

# Acknowledgements

Whilst the characters and organisations described in this book are entirely fictitious, I have nonetheless tried to depict Yorkshire and the textile industry as accurately as I can. The research was enormous fun, because the West Riding is full of larger than life people and places. I was able in the space of a morning to go from wild moorland to twenty-first century technology and then into a vast mill built over a hundred years ago where the past seems to be nudging at your shoulder. Many people were very kind and patient, taking the time to describe what are often complex processes in terms that I could understand. In particular I must thank Abraham Moons of Guiseley, Parkland Textiles of Apperley Bridge, Woolcombers, the Wool Marketing Board and the International Wool Secretariat. Let me stress that any disasters and inefficiencies I describe are the product of my imagination, with no reflection on the realities of life in these firms.

In addition I should like to express my gratitude to the many textile men who were kind enough to tell me what it is really like travelling to far-flung places buying and selling, although to them it is so everyday that they really couldn't work out why I wanted to know. I hope this book explains all.

# Chapter One

The warehouse roof was leaking. At some time during the storms of the past winter, rain had come in and soaked four or five bales of scoured wool. Since then they had sat and mouldered. Now, broken open on the floor, they spilled out their contents. The smell was disgusting, like sour dishcloths, and it was somebody's fault.

Andrew turned to the warehouseman. 'Which is it? Do we know?'

'Oh aye. It's the good stuff.'

Of course, it would be. Though why good wool had stood unused in the warehouse for months was beyond him, they might as well leave pound notes to go sodden in the rain. Did he have to do everything himself, from counting bales of wool to watching for leaks in the roof? 'Somebody should have told me,' he said loudly. 'Surely someone noticed?' The warehouseman eyed him inscrutably.

Andrew sighed. There was no point in making it worse. But what in God's name did they do now? Sinking his hands into his pockets, he said tightly: 'Can we send it back to the scourer? It might wash out.'

The warehouseman seemed almost insulted to be asked about something so far outside his experience. He said frostily, 'Buggered if I know. Might never get rid of the stink.'

For a minute Andrew thought about sending the wool through the mill as it was, if they could dye it navy blue they would almost match the mould. God knows what the workers would say though. Besides, they didn't need navy blue yarn, they needed piece-dyed orange cloth and they needed this wool to make it.

Stamping back through the warehouse, his feet splashing

in other, less damaging, puddles, he let the problem slip from his mind. Tomorrow, when he felt fresh, the solution would present itself. Pity they couldn't start on the order but there was just no telling when this sort of thing might happen and disrupt everything, especially with a firm like Judge's housed in a vast old mill that crumbled about them. Sometimes he dreamed of letting the whole shooting match burn down. Sometimes he dreamed of lighting the fire himself.

The clack of high heels sounded on the slate floor. He looked up expectantly, a smile already brightening his thin, serious face. He could always tell Diana's step, long and unhurried. She came in from the yard, holding her fur jacket close to her neck against the chill spring wind. He thought how lovely she was.

'Oh, there you are, Andrew, Frances said you were in here. Lunch. Don't say you've forgotten.'

His wife put up her cheek for him to kiss, a sure sign that she was still irritated with him. With a sense of glum horror he realised that he had forgotten to ask Frances to book a table, the morning's crisis had put it quite out of his mind. This lunch, intended as a peace-offering, might well degenerate into another squabble.

'Go and sit in the car, darling, I must wash my hands,' he said hurriedly. 'I won't be a tic, I promise.'

Diana sighed gustily.

He was gone a good ten minutes, because Frances couldn't find the number of the restaurant, and then couldn't get through. But there was a table, for which Andrew felt a profound relief. He ran across to his Jaguar and climbed in beside his wife.

'Sorry. Telephone call.' He reversed out of his parking space and swept through the high, wrought-iron gates that bore the inscription 'Isaac Judge Ltd.' in gold letters, into the narrow road where now and then the cobbles pushed their way back up through the tarmac. Within the space of this one road were two more mills, both empty, their chimneys pointing uselessly at the sky. They'd both gone down in the last ten years, beaten by shrinking markets supplied at give-away prices by Far Eastern sweatshops. Throughout it all, Judge's had held on. Their chimney still smoked, the orders dribbled in: for old lady skirtings, drab overcoats, sometimes a cheap grey flannel. Hanging on, waiting for the upturn that never seemed to come.

The car lifted its nose and sped up the hill, at once deserting the confines of the town and plunging into the country. That was the thing about Bradford, it was industry lapped all about by hills, moors, the cold blue Yorkshire air. The wind whistled in the rough grass. Sheep ran across the road in front of them.

Andrew opened the window and took in great gouts of air. Diana shuddered pointedly. He wound the window up again. 'Sorry, darling. I'll put the heater up.' Before he could reach the controls Diana did it, her long, thin fingers neat and precise. The silence in the car became almost solid.

Suddenly Andrew pulled the car hard on to the grass at the side of the road. Diana squeaked with fright, choking the sound off as they jerked to a halt.

'I'm sorry,' he said. 'You know I'm sorry.'

'You're always bloody sorry,' said Diana bitterly.

Andrew swallowed. 'I hate to hear you swear.'

'Well, I hate feeling so – let down.'

He reached across and put his hand over both of hers, where they twisted in her lap. 'Does it mean that much to you?' he asked, and her eyes blazed at him, amazed that he should even ask.

'You know it does! Honestly, Andrew, it isn't even as if I hadn't given up things to have it. My car's falling apart, I have to make up excuses every time Linda suggests we go clothes shopping, but I don't mind that! I just want my music room.'

'And a new violin for Andy,' muttered Andrew.

'Well of course! You weren't going back on that, were you? Not as well? He's got talent, he *has* to have a decent violin!'

3

His face worked desperately. 'Darling, I know he needs it, if I had the money do you think I wouldn't buy it today? And Rowan needs her skiing holiday with the school, and Sally needs a new bike — but with the firm as it is, there just isn't the spare cash.'

'Except for this nice new car.' A voice of cut glass.

'I've told you! If I don't have a new car, people will think we're going down,' insisted Andrew. 'We have to look as if we're doing well. No one's going to place orders if they think we're about to go out of business.'

'Well, build the music room and impress them,' snarled his wife. 'I've heard the same excuses ever since we moved into the blasted house, when the truth is you're jealous of my music and of Andy! You promised me and I've waited years and years, it isn't fair to spoil it now!'

She began to cry, angry tears of frustration and pain. A headache thumped at Andrew's brain. She was right, of course she was right, he did resent the love affair she had with her music, but not enough to deny her this. His mistake had been in letting her think the music room would be this year. She had rushed ahead with the plans, found a builder, talked to the gardener about moving the plants from the bed next to the house, everything. Like the craven he was, he had put off doing the sums, put off discussing it with her, until it was all much too late. And he couldn't bear to see her cry.

'Darling — if we changed the plans a little,' he ventured. 'Suppose we put up the basic structure and then did the inside as we can afford it?'

Her head came up. 'You mean — just the outside walls and things? I could still have my floor-length windows, couldn't I? And the vaulted ceiling?'

'Well, I suppose so.' Andrew was hurrying down his escape route. 'We'll do what we can, anyway. Perhaps Andy wouldn't mind waiting a few months for his new violin, his old one's not that bad —'

'He'll never win competitions with it,' interposed Diana, but her husband rushed on regardless.

4

' – and then we can finish if off gradually. I know it's not quite as you wanted, darling, but since you want it so much . . .'

Diana's eyes were brilliant in her pale face. She put out her arms and hugged her husband, enveloping him in her scent, her softness, her warmth. 'I'm sorry I was such a beast,' she whispered. 'I know it will cost a lot, but I want it desperately! I've waited so long, Andrew, I couldn't bear to be put off now. We can afford it, can't we?'

A brief vision of the bales of mouldy wool flashed into his head; half the weaving shed was standing idle waiting for the yarn to be spun from it, and with so thin an order book he ought to be travelling, ought to be getting business. Still, if he lied about a new order he should get a few bales of wool from the merchant, and some money might come in before he had to pay. And the mouldy wool would be worth something – but his wife didn't want to hear it. He bent his head and kissed her. 'You have just what you want.'

James Barton ran his fingers down the grain of panelled oak. It had come from a once prosperous mill and he had saved it, snatched it from under the noses of the liquidators, to line his office. The pleasure it gave him was un-diminished, partly because of its beauty, mostly because of his acumen.

Below, in the yard, they were unloading dyed yarn, and he considered going down to have a look at it. But he would soon hear if there was anything wrong, he had good men checking. It was just that he was restless today; there were things to be done and they needed doing, but nothing was urgent or unpredictable. When he had first grabbed Bardsey's from his father's incapable fingers, every day had been filled with knife-edge decisions that had to be right. He hadn't been able to sleep, he remembered, not through fear, because he had never feared anything, but excitement. They had been good times, stretching, growing times, when he had even managed to surprise himself.

Not that he slept very well nowadays. He supposed he was bored, though that was a slight word for what seemed like lead in his soul. Was it a year since he had first noticed it, first woken up and thought of the day and felt — bored? At night now he lay beside Marjorie as she murmured and snored, and wondered about the point of it all; all that striving and energy, struggle and brilliance, just to come to this. A plump wife, her lips shiny with nightcream; a house heavy with affluence, a son well established at a good school. In the dark of the small hours he asked himself, 'What now? Here you are, James Barton, you made it. What next?'

There was a perfunctory knock on the door and Saul came into the office. James at once transferred his irritation to him.

'What the hell do you want?'

Saul paused, but with his usual insouciance said cheerfully, 'God, you must have a hangover. I've brought the samples for you to look at.'

'So you have. Put them on the side table.'

James watched irritably as Saul went to obey. It was an interesting game, to see how much his brother would take before he acknowledged James's hostility, and fought back. Two or three times there had been monumental rows, but in the end Saul always came to heel. It was as if he hadn't the energy to spare for trivial things like position and power, preferring fast cars, fast women and amusement. Which, if nothing else, proved that very little of the same blood flowed in their veins.

They weren't even much alike in looks, for Saul was thicker, more muscled, his eyes a soft liquid brown that could turn the colour of autumn leaves. The two men were of a height though, well over six feet, but leaving that aside James wondered, not for the first time, if Saul was indeed his own father's son. Where was the pale skin and carrot hair that were James's legacy? Perhaps in the matter of paternity, as in so much else, old man Barton had been mis-

6

taken. Still, though he had accepted and provided for this late-born son, he hadn't made the even bigger mistake of marrying the mother.

'How was Spain? I see you managed to fit in your sunbathing.' James took a swipe at the tan he could never achieve and Saul managed almost all year round.

'I did some good business,' said Saul casually. 'And like a fool I made the mistake of going to see a bullfight, a real local *corrida*. I don't say the bloke wasn't brave, but when they skewered the poor beast I was an inch from throwing up. The lady I was with wasn't amused.'

'Who was she? A contact, I hope.'

'A daughter of one of the customers. Pretty as anything but the soul of Lucrezia Borgia. I ruined my chances by suggesting she start a campaign to abolish the bullfight – which seems to be tantamount to a call for the compulsory castration of all Spanish men. Don't look so alarmed! I sent her a leather handbag the next day. At the moment she wants to marry me.'

James snorted. An endless queue of ladies wanted to marry Saul, but he seemed to be able to avoid it and keep them happy. It was one of his major talents.

'If we could talk about work?' he said patiently.

'Anything you like, brother mine. Thought you were more interested in rending my living flesh, but even you must get bored with it.'

He was right. Today nothing could lighten James's mood.

Saul began expertly spreading out the sample cloth on the table. Clearly it was something he had done many times before, but the colours themselves were startlingly fresh: purple and orange and bright green. Saul set them out in interesting combinations, filling the centre with a matt-black coat material, dense and flat. They had produced it on a hunch of James's because he had seen a calf-length black coat at a tacky London fashion event and for him it had rung bells.

'Looks good,' said James, shining a torch on the orange.

7

The shade changed, taking on a bluish tint. 'Couldn't we get this better?' he demanded. 'Women's suiting, isn't it? You know how the bloody shops complain, all those housewives and typists bringing things back because they thought it would match the blouse and now it doesn't seem to. You did notice it, I suppose?'

'Not exactly my department,' retorted Saul. 'All I do is sell the stuff. I mean, if you want me to pop back from New York, or even Tokyo, and check the dye then I'll be delighted. Of course you're just round the corner, and an innocent might think it would be easier for you, but anything to oblige.'

'Oh, you're so bloody funny,' said James sourly. He knew perfectly well that they had settled on the inferior dye because not only did it cost less but thankfully did not come off on the skin, as did the more expensive stuff whatever they tried. They needed to put some real money into researching dyes; he would have to brace himself and do it despite the unprofitable time it would take.

The thought depressed him still further. Determined to rile Saul he said, 'You should consider letting someone else do some of the long trips; I've mentioned it to you before.'

The brown eyes fixed on him, but for once Saul was silent. They both knew that James was threatening him with the loss of his job, and if there was one single thing in the world Saul cared about it was that. A brilliant, inspired salesman, his biggest thrill was using the world as his backyard. He was that rare and almost extinct species, a natural traveller. Luxury hotel or mud-floored hovel, it was all the same to him.

He spoke six languages, knew personally most of the stewardesses on the long-haul routes and could just as easily chat up the lady owner of a Chinese junk. He went to China nowadays to buy raw silk, and to sell cloth, but unless specifically requested he wouldn't bore you with tales of silk farms where the worms hung for weeks in humid sheds and women sat all day unravelling the cocoons. The satisfaction was for himself alone, and for James to hurt him irrevocably he had only to take away his job. Thankfully not even James could afford to lose him — yet.

They went through the samples, comparing weights and prices, discussing lead times on orders.

'It's all very new,' said Saul doubtfully. 'It's a risk. Perhaps we should play safe and combine it with some of the old range.'

'I think not.' It was James's turn to be adventurous. 'After all, we're selling a look, not a ragbag of styles. We'll push the new range first, we can send someone else out with the old faithfuls.'

'When I've fallen flat on my face with this,' retorted Saul. But he knew he wouldn't. It was good and it was of the times, and as usual James was right. How he hated to admit it.

Unexpectedly, James went to the drinks cabinet and poured them both a whisky. Surprised and somewhat mollified, Saul took his. An uncomfortable silence fell and Saul hunted about for something to say. James's threat had rattled him badly. Finally he said, 'I met Joss Wainwright for lunch; he's trying to tempt us with South African tops again.' Every now and then someone who didn't understand the situation at Bardsey's lunched Saul under the mistaken impression that he had something to do with the running of the firm.

'Tell him to get his quality right, then we'll talk,' commented James.

'That's what I said to him. Andrew Judge was there — wife in a fur coat, new Jag in the car park.'

'Good God!' James was honestly surprised. 'And I thought they were starving to death. That firm's gone downhill ever since the old man died.'

'In such marked contrast to Bardsey's,' said Saul thinly. It could not be said that his fortunes had improved since the death of Frederick Barton. At least while he was alive Saul could believe in the fiction that the firm would one day be shared between the two sons, disregarding the small matter of his illegitimacy. Afterwards Saul saw exactly where he stood, which was in the same place as his mother, the house-keeper, on an unmarked spot between the Promised Land and the Wilderness.

'Would you say Judge's was a sound firm?' asked James suddenly.

Saul shrugged. 'Produces good cloth of its type. At least it did. These days it's falling apart. I wouldn't have thought we need concern ourselves.'

'Supplies the cheaper end though, doesn't it? Undercuts us by pounds per yard.'

'If that's what you like. We're a quality firm, James, Bardsey's quality worsted, and Judge's is a little woollen outfit paddling around in a pond. They don't compete with us!' He watched his brother closely. 'What are you after?'

Draining the dregs of whisky, James said, 'Whatever it is, it has nothing to do with you. Are you going to stand around here drinking all day or can I expect to see your usual ridiculous expenses claim some time this year? I must be paying for half the champagne in France!'

Saul allowed himself a slight grin and gathered up his samples. 'I never drink French wine in Spain, it upsets the natives. Tact, James, tact. Not that I need to tell you about that!'

The door closed behind him, and despite himself James felt himself grinning. Thoughtfully he chewed the inside of his cheek. Suddenly he felt restricted and enclosed, he couldn't breathe. The office was too hot; outside in the yard a fork lift truck was whining with the persistence of a drill. He had to get out into the air, to clear his head of whisky and dullness. Grabbing his coat from the cupboard, he strode from the room.

# Chapter Two

James took the Mercedes up to Shipley Glen. Nobody was there on such a brisk weekday, and he parked and wandered amongst the stiff, barely sprouting bilberry. He wanted to walk but not alone; he wouldn't have minded taking his son Richard with him, except that he was away at school. He wanted — something. What a curse had fallen upon him, to have the world offered to him on a plate and to desire none of it. He supposed he could travel, but unlike Saul he loathed the planes and the food, the hotel bedrooms and the stench of street markets. His mind turned back to what had so often been his consolation in the past, his only consolation: work, deals, money. He thought of Judge's.

It was doing better than might be expected, it seemed, and he could almost envy Andrew Judge, a man he knew but slightly. For him the struggle was still before him, the battle yet to be won. Each day would bring its own new challenges, the hours rushing by on a charge of adrenaline. How he would like to be running that firm!

He thought about the two concerns. Bardsey's was essentially in worsteds, using the long flat fibres of fine wools to make smooth, quality cloth. In the past they had prospered on men's suiting, but the advent of casual wear had put a dent in that market. They were more versatile now.

Judge's was a woollen firm, taking the lesser quality, short fibres of a fleece and spinning them into fluffy yarn for tweeds and cheaper stuff. Unlike Bardsey's, who designed and wove the cloth, leaving almost everything else to outside firms, Judge's did everything, from the raw wool to the dyeing and finishing of the fabric, all under the same roof. It was both a strength and a weakness. If you had everything under your own control, you didn't rely on others to meet your deadlines. But if times were hard, you had capacity, and people, you couldn't use. James had been thinking about diversification for a long time. That yarn today had arrived late from a commission spinner. Bardsey's didn't have enough control at that end, they were left apologising for late deliveries that were nothing to do with them. Suppose they owned the spinner? And the dye-house, and the finishing plant, perhaps even the firm that took the sheared wool and combed it, the whole damned shooting match? Suppose they owned even a little woollen concern to mop up the other end of the market? Research needed a spread of applications to make it worthwhile, so in a way he would be justifying that investment. The risks were considerable, it would be difficult and expensive, but surely it would not be boring. That had to be the first consideration.

He turned and began to stride back to his car, his heavy coat whirling around him. A crow, hopping about on the grass, shrieked and flapped slowly into the air. James picked up a pebble and threw it after the bird, sending the stone high into the cold blue sky. Today, without wasting time, he would go and look at Judge's and see for himself.

Although they didn't finish lunch until half-past three, Andrew insisted that he must go back to work, for half an hour at least. Diana decided to wait for him; she hated to see the harassed look that came upon him when she was difficult and work was difficult, and in general she tried not to add to his problems. Sometimes, though, he had to be pushed. Andrew wasn't a very positive person and on occasion she had to insist on things. He could be too kind and gentle for anyone's good.

Andy would be on his way to his music lesson now. When the music room was built she would insist that his teacher came to the house, it was too exhausting for the child to trail around here, there and everywhere. One thing she wouldn't compromise on was adequate sound-proofing; she could not bear Rowan and Sally to intrude with their blaring television, and then to complain about Andy's scales. Girls were awkward beings, Rowan especially. Diana clashed with her elder daughter almost daily, about clothes or tidiness, and mostly Rowan's impossible jealousy of Andy. Undoubtedly he received a great deal of time and attention, but he was the one with the talent. Rowan must learn to accept it.

To pass the time, she strolled up and down the long oak-floored corridor that overlooked the yard. When she first met Andrew it was lined with paintings, there was silver in the boardroom and Crown Derby on the tea tray. All that had been swallowed up, poured down the throat of the mill because at all costs the creature must be kept alive. Why? Why hadn't they sold out years ago, when they still had money, when Andrew was young and drove a two-seater and made jokes that delighted her?

A Mercedes drove into the yard, the numberplate JB.1. Everyone in Bradford knew that number, it was the whiz kid of Bardsey's, the man they called lucky because no one knew how he did it. She watched him step from the car. Tall, with carroty hair and pale, almost white, skin. The men in the yard wiped their hands on their trousers and sent messages, while James Barton put his hands in his pockets and stared up at the windows. He had rather prominent grey eyes. Diana stepped back.

Andrew, obviously flustered, came hurrying out of his office. Diana turned to him. 'Darling, isn't that James Barton?'

'Seems so. Wonder what he wants.' Andrew straightened his tie nervously, clearing his throat with his habitual tense cough.

'Is he coming up?'

'I said I'd go down. Come on, darling, you can meet him too.'

13

They went down the wide staircase, once polished daily but now dull and cobwebbed. Andrew hurried across to greet Barton but Diana, with some instinct of pride, took her leisurely time.

'Andrew!' Barton was holding out his hand. 'Good to see you after so long.'

'Good to see you too, James.' Andrew had hardly been aware that Barton even knew him. 'May I introduce my wife – Diana, James Barton.' Barton automatically extended his hand, only to find it ignored. Diana inclined her head graciously, remaining at some distance. Andrew almost hiccupped.

'What can I do for you, James?'

He was too eager. It would have been better to let Barton make the approach. James said, 'To be honest, Andrew, I really wanted to have a look round. Please, say no if you'd rather I didn't, but I just felt – well, there might be some business in it. There's a future for your type of cloth.'

The colour came and went in Andrew's face and he glanced towards his wife, as if for reassurance. Diana stared at Barton. 'It's hardly convenient today, Andrew,' she said thinly.

'Well – let's make it convenient,' said Andrew. 'You don't mind, do you, darling? Go and wait upstairs if you'd rather.' He ushered Barton towards the buildings, but for some reason James stopped.

He turned to Diana and said in an odd voice; 'I hope I'm not spoiling your day. Forgive me if I am.'

They looked at each other. She could see a pulse beating under the pale skin of his forehead. In a softer tone she murmured, 'Perhaps we can spare half an hour.'

As the men went into the warehouse, James said, 'What a beautiful woman your wife is.'

'Yes.' In that one word Andrew encapsulated all the surprise that had never abated, despite three children and years of marriage, in his capture of a woman as beautiful

14

and talented as Diana. As the years went by and she acquired elegance and style, he found himself marvelling more and more. At dinner parties he looked at her white neck and glossy auburn hair, echoed in huge gold-flecked eyes, and wondered how on earth he had come to be married to her.

'Odd smell you have in here,' said James.

'Nothing serious,' replied Andrew quickly, rushing him past the mouldy bales. He had forgotten them, or he would have brought the visitor another way.

All at once he saw the place through a stranger's eye: the disorder, the odd parcel of camel or deer hair that had been left over from a job and never used since, the puddles, and above all the stink. Yet Barton said nothing.

They passed the boiler-room, where the monolithic coal-eating monster that supplied the mill's needs rumbled and coughed. Barton stopped for an unscheduled look, though Andrew couldn't imagine why. 'We're not very up to date in here, I'm afraid,' he apologised. 'But it works.' A fine film of dust lay over everything, the boilermen looked like miners at the end of a shift. Andrew almost dragged his visitor on into the mill.

Inevitably one of the cards was stopped. Judge's carding machines, designed to bring order to the tangled mass of fibres in a fleece so that it could be spun, were getting on in years. So was the man who cared for them, and heaven knows who would keep them going once he retired.

'All right, Nobby?' he yelled.

Nobby, long since deafened and as always armed with screwdriver and oily rag, scanned the visitor. 'Oh aye, sir. We'll have it going soon, sir, that we will.' Word of the visitor had travelled and he was on best behaviour. Throughout the mill figures could be seen suddenly sweeping up and getting on. Judge's was doing its best to look presentable, but nothing could give work to idle looms. In the old days it was impossible to talk in here with the roar of hundreds of sheds clattering up and down.

'We're about to start a big new order,' hastened Andrew. 'We want to keep clear for it.'

'Very wise,' said Barton. Was there a hint of irony there? Hard to tell.

They went on, through the dye-house where a cauldron of grey cloth bubbled and foamed, and overflowed on to the floor, into the burling and mending department where women sat in a north light all day, mending faults in the weave. Perhaps the light made it seem drabber than need be. Rolls and rolls of dull fabrics, most of it quite well made but old-fashioned and uninspired.

Andrew stopped at a coarse green cloth. 'One of our new designs,' he said doubtfully. Even he didn't think it looked very new. Judge's had been making a variation on that pattern since his father took over.

Barton suddenly seemed impatient. He pulled his hands from his pockets and made for the door. 'Sorry to have taken up so much of your time. Good to see you're doing well, Andrew.'

Andrew, long legs loping beside him, said, 'I suppose we're lucky to have made it through the last ten years really. That must say something.'

James almost laughed. Yes, he thought to himself, it says that your father was a damn sight better at this job than you are. The only thing that's kept you going these last ten years is the money he made, and there should have been better ways of spending it. Aloud he said, 'I'll just say goodbye to your wife, if I may? I should apologise for disrupting your afternoon.'

Diana was in Andrew's office, idly leafing through an old copy of *Country Life*. The desk was disordered, the open shelves behind cluttered with papers and unread magazines. Wool samples gathered dust on top of a filing cabinet. 'God,' thought James. 'God Almighty.'

He turned and met Diana's large tawny eyes and suddenly he didn't know what to say. They looked at each other with complete understanding. She put the magazine back on the table and idly ran her finger through the dust. He swallowed. 'I just came to say — goodbye.'

She spread her hands. 'Well then — goodbye.' It was tempered with a slight smile and, encouraged, he said: 'Don't be too cross with me. I know I ruined your day.'

'Oh no.' Diana folded her magazine and got up, moving to stand beside her husband. She took his upper arm in both her hands and James thought, 'She knows that's annoying me.' She smiled back at him and said coolly, 'Today couldn't be spoiled. Andrew's agreed to build my music room. That may not sound much to you but I've waited for it for years.'

'Diana plays the violin,' explained Andrew. 'She's quite brilliant.'

Diana wrinkled her nose, the one slightly imperfect feature in her face. It had a slight hook to it. 'Not at all,' she murmured. 'My son is the one with the brilliance.'

James said, 'I wish I could hear you both play.'

Back in his car and driving out of the narrow gate, James looked in his mirror and saw Andrew standing uncertainly, watching him. He felt suddenly drunk, though he had only had the one whisky with Saul. He was almost glad to get away, out of that sour-smelling, doomed mill, away from the cool sensuality of Judge's wife. She disturbed him.

He drove on for a while and then stopped next to a row of derelict shops. Judge's was a mess, out of date, over-manned, disorganised. They would survive only as long as their flimsy facade of prosperity remained intact. He could destroy it and them tomorrow if he wished, just by a few casual words. 'Judge's? On their knees, old boy. Went round the other day, place is a bloody shambles. Might have a new car but he sodding well can't afford it.'

If it had been a fraction less bad he might have bought them out. As it was he would leave them to stew and in a few months, perhaps a year or two, Judge's would be on the scrap heap and that would be that.

'It's all so bloody unfair.' He spoke out loud, bitterly. Because tonight Andrew Judge, that long lanky incompetent, was going home with his beautiful wife. She knew what her husband was but today she was delighted with him because he was spending money she knew he couldn't afford. Those pale legs, that she crossed and uncrossed so seductively, would be well and truly open tonight, and it seemed to James, suddenly, that Andrew Judge had the one thing that he, James Barton, wanted.

# Chapter Three

Diana put on her old woollen jacket and stepped out into the garden. The daffodils were waving gaily in the breeze, in other years she had picked them, brought them into every room in the house, called the children to see how pretty they were. Not this year, not in her present mood. She felt a rising tide of bitterness. She walked quickly down the path, stopped under the beech tree and turned to look at the house. Now she could see exactly how bad things were.

In her mind's eye she had pictured an octagonal building linked to the main house by a narrow spur of brickwork, and that was what she had planned and the architect had drawn. It would have been gracious, sunny and beautiful. This rectangle, still mercifully only three feet high, was nothing like her intention. She felt unreasoning rage.

Marching back up the garden, she cursed the builder, the workmen, and most of all Andrew. He was the one who had demanded the changes, and presumably agreed this emasculation of the project. How on earth could he permit this monstrosity to be fixed to the house, like a pimple, like a ghastly suburban garage? She aimed a spiteful kick at one of the walls, and to her surprise it wobbled. The mortar was still damp, it was only an hour or two since the bricklayer left, driven away by her fierce complaints.

'Right,' she muttered and looked round for an implement. One of the pieces of timber they used for shuttering concrete was lying on the ground. She picked it up, wielded it like a cricket bat and hit the wall. Only two bricks fell off, so she hit it twice more, and then leaned against the house and pushed with her feet. That was very effective. She

19

breached an entire hole and what was left tilted crazily.

'That's making a terrible mess of your shoe.'

She spun round, scarlet with surprise and shock. James Barton stood at the French windows, watching her.

'How did you get in ?'

'The front door was open. I'm sorry, I thought something might be wrong.'

Diana snorted and turned back to the mess of bricks around her. 'You were right. God, but I hate it,' she said unnecessarily.

James stood in silence and Diana aimed another vicious kick at the wall, then another, and another. He reached out quickly, and grabbed her arms. 'Don't. Please — don't.'

Diana pulled free and brushed away angry tears. 'Just come and look,' she hissed and pulled herself free. She started back down the garden and James followed, thinking that he was in the presence of a mad woman. But how he loved to touch her.

When she stopped, he turned obediently and looked back at the house. Even he, who lived in a house she would certainly despise, could see how unsuitable the embryo building would be. Non-committal, James said, 'Not at all what I would have chosen.'

'Don't think I chose it,' snapped Diana. 'The plan was for an octagon, with a vaulted roof and floor-length windows leading out on to the lawn. I'd rather not have anything than — this!' Her gesture encompassed everything, all her frustration and anger.

'Shall I knock it down for you?' asked James.

The tawny eyes turned on him like twin cannon. 'Yes.'

He tore the wall down with his bare hands, brick by brick. Diana stood and watched him, her face as set as that of an angry goddess. When he had finished and the bricks lay in a jumble of half-set mortar, James panted: 'Will that do?'

'Yes. Thank you.'

He was breathing hard, there was mud on his trousers and

20

a graze on one hand. Was that all she would say: 'thank you'?

They went into the house. Diana put the kettle on, saying, 'I suppose you're looking for Andrew. He's in London this week.'

'Is he? Damn.'

'Didn't his secretary tell you that?'

'No, she didn't.' Although she might have done had he asked her. He was only here because someone had mentioned that Judge was going to town for a few days. He hadn't intended to come really. Somehow he just had.

While she waited for the kettle, Diana took off her shoe and studied the heel. The leather was badly scratched. 'What a mistake it is to let temper get the better of you,' she said ruefully.

To her surprise, James reached out and took the shoe from her. 'I'll see to it for you.'

'We can still afford shoe repairs, I can assure you.'

'Really, I have some shoes to take in myself. I'll bring it back tomorrow. We can lunch.'

Diana shook her head. 'I couldn't.'

'Please.' James came a little closer, bending his head to her confidingly. 'I'd like to talk about Judge's. I'm sure you can tell me as much as Andrew, if not more. He's too close to it.'

Glancing up with a long-necked flick of her hair she said, 'I may as well admit it, I hate the place. It's a great big fly that needs feeding all the time. All that grubbing and struggling. Why do you men bother with it?'

She fixed him with her clear gaze and he stared back. 'I don't know,' he said with sudden honesty. 'It used to excite me.'

'But not any more.'

'No.'

She moved away and made the tea, her stockinged foot balanced on the toes.

21

James felt a surge of emotion for that poised, slender foot. He said, 'I'll pick you up at twelve.'

'Oh God, if you must. How I hate talking about that damned firm.' She passed him a mug of tea. Marjorie always presented a visitor with a cup, she didn't know how to be casual. She put on her pearls just to go down to the supermarket and she kept her house, too, on permanent best behaviour. Here there was attractive disorder. Misty flowered wallpaper, and on the polished wood of the hall floor a couple of worn Persian rugs. Marjorie woud have got rid of those years ago.

They said nothing, but Diana seemed unconcerned by the silence. At last James finished his tea and put the mug down. 'Don't mention this to Andrew just yet,' he said briskly. 'We don't want to raise his hopes.'

'All right' said Diana. 'Look, I must go and change my shoes, I have to collect my son in half an hour. Can you see yourself out?'

'I saw myself in,' said James.

'So you did.'

She was gone, and he stood alone in the kitchen, holding the shoe. He ran his fingers over the torn leather.

He arrived at the house twenty minutes early the next day, the shoe on the seat beside him. Switching off the engine, he stared at the building, or at least all he could see through the thick screen of laurel and conifer, elm and beech. Like Judge himself it was restrained and out of its time. A good house to live in, though.

After ten minutes he started the car again and drove the last twenty yards up to the front door. It was shut this time, and there was no sign of life within. The sharp thud of disappointment in his gut took him by surprise, he almost grunted. Instead he went to the door and rapped on it forcefully, and in a few moments he heard soft footfalls in the hall. Diana stood there, in stockinged feet, wearing a silk blouse and the pencil skirt of what was probably a suit if she had had time to put on the jacket.

'You're far too early. I've hardly begun to get dressed.'

'Come as you are.' He laughed, but choked it off as her face stiffened. She wasn't ready for that sort of informality. Quickly he added, 'We're only going to talk business.'

'I think at least I should brush my hair,' she said.

Leaving him there, she went quickly back through the hall and up the wide staircase. James had a vision of following her, rushing after her into the bedroom. The urge was so strong he actually took the first step. He circled his wrist with the fingers of his other hand and squeezed. What was he doing here, why was he making such a fool of himself? Suppose she told Judge all about this when he came home?

So far there was nothing to tell. Besides, Judge was a nobody on the road to nowhere who had nothing to recommend him but his beautiful — so beautiful — wife.

Diana descended the stairs again at twenty past twelve. James had booked the restaurant for half-past. 'Do you always take so long?' he asked, because he never allowed himself to be kept waiting.

Diana confounded him by replying. 'I really couldn't say,' she said. 'I take as long as I need. It would be silly otherwise, because if I wasn't dressed properly I shouldn't enjoy my lunch. Would you rush out half-shaved because the clock said eight o'clock, and then spend the whole day looking ridiculous?'

James was taken aback. He moved mentally into a higher gear, even then could think of nothing to say and fell back on a compliment. 'Beautiful women don't need to spend hours getting ready.' She cast him a sideways look out of her wide tawny eyes. 'I cannot agree. Beauty is a fragile plant and it dies without nourishment.'

In the car she picked up the shoe and studied it briefly. 'Why, thank you. Where did you take it?'

He grinned. 'A man I know.' He hadn't known him

23

before yesterday, a little Pakistani cobbler working from a rundown shop in the Asian district of Bradford. No one else had been open at that time. Diana tossed the shoe on to the back seat of the car and waited for James to drive away. He forced himself to stop watching her and do so.

They lunched at a country pub, on steak and kidney pie. James had never been there before but the smart places were all frequented by textile men and they would have been seen. To make up, he bought a half bottle of champagne. Diana put her elegant elbow on the table, rested her chin on her hand and stared at him. 'Why are you doing this? You don't give a damn about Judge's.'

He held her glass under her chin for the bubbles to tickle her. 'I don't know if that's true. At the moment I'm just enjoying your company.'

'What do you mean?'

She disconcerted him every time she opened her mouth. He heard himself say, 'You excite me. You make me feel alive.'

And she nodded, understanding him. 'It's terrible to go through life half-asleep. Most people do, you know, most of the time.'

'Do you?'

'I have my music.'

She hadn't mentioned Andrew Judge. Did he bore her the way Marjorie bored him? When she lay beneath him at night was it the reverse of him and Marjorie, he dutifully poking a weak erection in and out of her flab?

Diana said, 'You're very rich, aren't you?'

'No. I've made money, I'm good at it. I could be very rich if I went on. But when I talk to you I realise I haven't done anything else, there isn't anything else to me. I'm ashamed of that.'

'Why?' Diana smiled at him. It was a soft, open smile that she only allowed herself when she knew she was the victor. She felt this man bowing down to her.

24

'I'm ashamed of not making more of my life.'

Her smile disappeared. She said, 'I feel that, too, you know. There are so many things I want to do, but I can't let myself do them. I feel cooped up here, I feel trapped!'

'You mean your music, don't you? You could have been famous.'

She flared at him, almost vicious. 'You don't know anything about it! I could be terrible, you don't know that I'm not. Everybody always wants genius. They don't want to live next door to a quite good player, they don't want to know if someone's just a hundred times better than most, they want them to be the best ever, the only talent, the new Mozart! I'm not that wonderful. I'm just very good.'

James swallowed. Flattery wasn't the way to Diana's heart — if that was where he wanted to go. Where was he going? 'You're right,' he admitted. 'But I don't know a damn thing about music, it's one of the things I never got round to. Your son's good though, isn't he? Didn't you say that?'

He watched her anger dissolve away. 'Oh yes. Andy's wonderful. Much better than I was at his age. One day he just might be the best, but people never understand how much it costs, not in money but in dedication! And it's got to be worth it. I mean, suppose he was giving up his childhood, giving up football and carpentry and just the luxury of doing nothing, to devote himself to playing an instrument he's never going to be brilliant at? That would be such a waste, there'd be nothing to make up for it. Andrew doesn't understand that whatever it costs financially it isn't anything. He never sees the more important thing, he gets sidetracked by the girls wanting holidays and the bloody, bloody bank! God, I get sick of it all. It's hard enough without all these other things.'

She fell silent, twirling her glass, and James watched her intently. He could see that some inner spring had unwound a few turns, easing her temper and her nerves. 'This is important to me, you know,' he said.

She shook her head. 'It's one of the things we're not allowed. Important people come in clearly labelled boxes, and you haven't got a box for me.' Then she looked at him. 'But we can be unimportant to each other.'

The waitress came and asked if they would like pudding, and they shook their heads without looking at her. 'The bill, please,' said James. 'We must be going.'

Outside in the car he said, 'We could go somewhere. If you wanted.'

She sat with her hands braced against the dashboard, long slender hands with hard strength in the fingers. 'I don't know what I want. Have you got a wife? You have, haven't you?'

'Oh yes. And a son, I've got a son, Richard. I've never done this sort of thing before, I want you to know that. But, my God, Diana, you make me feel so alive!'

She breathed deeply through her nose. 'As long as you remember that we aren't important. That is what I want, James.'

He drove the quiet car into the quiet lane, taking it softly up the tree-lined drive. 'Nobody here,' he murmured.

'Not today, no.'

James said, 'I'm coming in.' He got out of the car and went round to her side, pulling open the door. She stared up at him. After a moment he reached across and unfastened her seat belt, smelling her perfume, the scent of her hair. He grabbed her arm and pulled her out of the car and she came, long-legged and unresisting. But when he tried to kiss her she turned away. He let her go.

She walked to the house, fumbling in her bag for her key and leaving the door swinging when she had opened it. James followed her inside, thinking, 'How can she do this to me, how can she be so bloody cruel?' He would do anything if she would just − could just − it would be enough to caress her bare feet!

She threw down her bag on a chair, her coat on the floor, walking through the house as if she were alone. James, hating himself for his subservience, followed. She entered a small, cluttered room, piled high with music, a piano crammed against one wall, a collapsing sofa against another and music stands like spiked insects in the centre of the floor. As James watched, she opened a violin case, took out the instrument and tuned it briefly.

'I don't need a damned music lesson!' he cried, but she didn't look at him. Her long arms in their silk blouse moved with heartbreaking grace, her head tilted to send her shining hair in a fall against her cheek. The music began.

He was assailed by it. The notes crashed out at him, rivers of them, torrents foaming against the walls of the room. She wrenched chords from the depths, plucked shrieks from the heavens, built a wall of sound within which she stood, exposed. Her teeth were clenched. There were tears glistening at the corners of her eyes. James took off his jacket and threw it down, pulled off his tie and discarded it. He went to her. He knelt on the worn carpet and embraced her, pushed his face into the fabric of her skirt, caressing her narrow bottom, feeling her knees shaking against his chest. She played on, harder, desperately. His fingers unfastened her skirt. He drew it down, exposing her white lace slip. He hooked his fingers in at her waist and stripped her.

The playing faltered and went on. He put his nose into wiry auburn hair, grunting with the pleasure of it. The smell of her, the heat. He placed his hands flat against her belly, reaching his square thumbs out to probe. Her bow slid wildly, she played a last wild screeching note. 'No! For God's sake no!' But she stood there for him. His two thumbs padded gently against her. It was so, so quiet. When she screamed it was like an animal in pain.

She took no part in what came after. He pushed her

down, mounted her, and she watched him as if in shock. Afterwards, too, when his head was spinning, when pleasure drugged him, she said nothing, did nothing. When he went, he left her lying on the old sofa.

# Chapter Four

Perhaps it would have been better if Andrew had been furious about the demolished music room. As it was, when he came back from his trip, his understanding, his sorrow, his apologies, all increased Diana's irritation. She deserved anger, she wasn't the paragon he imagined, she was a wilful, faithless woman aware of nothing but her selfish needs.

In a fit of temper she declared, 'I don't want the music room! Not like this! Why do you always try and keep everyone happy? In the end you make everyone miserable. God, Andrew, you can be so indecisive.'

'Darling, please!' But it was said to her retreating back. Did that mean he should recall the builders, or not? It was just one amidst many problems.

But, unaccountably, business was improving. One or two unexpected orders had come his way, from people he had never done business with before, which was very encouraging. At tea he said to Diana, 'Let's have another go at the music room with another builder. If we get the orders out on time we should have some spare cash.'

Rowan, pert and cheeky at fifteen, said, 'You should put the money back in the firm, Dad, you know you should. We don't need a music room.'

'Jealous,' said Andy unemotionally. He was a plump thirteen year old, calm and sensible, capable of getting himself up at six to practise, voluntarily forgoing the school trip because it clashed with a music lesson.

'Your mother wants the music room,' said Andrew firmly. 'It's decided.'

'No it isn't,' snapped Diana, putting her fingers to her

29

head. 'If the money should go into the business, then it should. At least then we wouldn't have to flinch every time there's a letter from the bank.'

'Please, darling, not in front of the children,' murmured her husband.

'It's all right, Dad,' chipped in Sally, the youngest at ten. 'We understand all about it. Miss Rogers says that all the mills that ought to go out of business have gone out of business. Everybody else is going to be O.K.'

'Not just because Miss Rogers says so,' sneered Rowan. 'Honestly, you don't understand anything. All those foreign peasants are working away in the Far East making things much cheaper than we can and putting us out of business. It isn't fair!'

Andrew took a scone and buttered it enthusiastically. 'Well, it depends on how you look at it, Rowan. Just think, when the mills here were built we were flooding the market with cheap goods and putting everyone else out of business. How can we complain now?'

'Because it's us!' declared his daughter. 'Besides, they don't make things nearly as well as we do.'

'Darling, people don't want wonderfully made things any more,' broke in Diana. 'They used to wear heavy suits and coats and trousers, but now it's all jeans and T-shirts. Look at your own clothes, hardly a wool dress to be seen.'

'I'll buy one tomorrow,' said Rowan, flinging her arms wide dramatically. She had her mother's long arms, but her father's dark colouring. 'Made in Britain!'

'We can't afford it,' said Andrew, looking comically lugubrious. Everyone laughed.

Returning home after the morning chaos of the school run, Diana wandered round the garden. The wreck of the music room kept catching her eye, but she knew she had been right to cause it. Ugliness proliferated when you let down your guard; it had to be fought against, resisted, even when you were too tired and preoccupied almost to notice. The sound of the vacuum came from inside the house, the daily doing her usual inadequate best. Restlessness nagged, and Diana refused to consider why. Guilt lurked in a corner of her mind and she hated it, because she did not feel it was justified. She had needed James Barton for herself, it had nothing to do with the family or Andrew or indeed Judge's. Although it was passing strange that the orders had come in just when Barton most wanted to impress her . . . She liked the way he looked at her, as if he was stalking a deer, trying this way, then that, never diverted from his purpose.

There was the sound of a car in the drive and she went through to see who it was. Glancing out of the window she saw James Barton standing before the door, her shoe held in his hand.

'I'll get it,' called Diana quickly as the vacuum droned to silence. She waited until it had begun again and then confronted her visitor.

'I've been meaning to bring this round,' said James. 'You left it in the car.'

'Thank you.' She did not ask him in.

'I wouldn't mind some coffee.'

'My daily's here. Besides, I don't want to see you again.'

He grimaced. 'I hope that's not true. I know we ought not to see each other again, but that's not the same thing at all.'

The daily woman switched off her machine and came clumping downstairs with her head swivelled in curiosity towards the visitor.

'I did hope your husband would be home, Mrs. Judge,' said James. 'But I'm sure I can explain the problem to you if you have the time.'

'Not really,' said Diana. Then, as the daily stood and James stood, she gave in. 'Perhaps I can spare ten minutes.'

In the kitchen James said, 'I hear things are a bit better at Judge's.'

She gave him a cold stare. 'I knew it was you. I didn't need paying.'

'Don't be stupid, please! I wanted to give you the world that afternoon, more than the world, but I couldn't even send you flowers. So I tried to give you your music room. I keep hearing your music in my head, it was — such an experience! All of it, the music, you —' He tailed off, shaking his head inadequately.

Suddenly fervent, she turned to him. 'I know! For me, too, I think. We should leave it at that, one afternoon we'll never forget. Somehow, I don't know why, I'd lost my sensuality. You gave it back to me.'

James put his hand on her arm, a hot hard touch. 'Not for him I didn't! For me! I've been dead half my life, I didn't understand feeling! I need more, Diana. I've never had it. I thought I knew what there was and I hadn't begun to explore. You've got to take me further. Don't give it to him!'

She turned her head and caught sight of the daily standing in the doorway.

'Shall I do the lounge?' asked the woman quickly.

'The drawing-room? Yes, please,' said Diana in the dismissive tone of one who has always employed help in the house. James wondered if he would like Marjorie better if she too had no lounge, but a drawing-room instead. As the woman went off he said, 'We can't talk here. Let's lunch. We can go to the same pub.'

'Don't be silly, you know we can't. We mustn't.'

'We have once, what difference would it make? We're both adults, we know it won't stay like this forever. I wake at night thinking about your breasts, I've never seen your breasts! Just once more. Something fantastic. On the moors, naked in the heather.'

She said slowly, 'Last night I dreamed you were making love to me. I knew I should stop you but I couldn't.'

James said, 'What time does the woman go?' Diana cast her eyes down. 'Twelve.'

When he had gone, she went upstairs to her room and closed the door. Last night when she had dreamed of James, Andrew had woken her. They had made love, in the gentle, respectful way that was typical of her husband, and it had satisfied her, gently. Why was she now burning for this other man? He pretended kindness but he wasn't kind. But then, neither was she. Each responded to the other's selfishness.

She put on a cream wool dress that fell high-necked from shoulder to knee. Underneath she wore nothing and her nipples stood out against the cloth. Twelve o'clock came and the daily went. Minutes later the Mercedes drew up at the door.

'I watched to see her go,' said James. 'I couldn't wait.' He was wearing jeans and an open-necked shirt. His grey eyes gleamed with excitement. Already his erection bulged stiffly beneath his belt. On the back seat of the car rested a bottle of champagne, two glasses, several packs of salmon and prawn sandwiches and two large rugs.

'You're very organised,' said Diana, settling herself into the car.

'Everything runs better with organisation,' said James, and grinned wolfishly.

They drove high on to the moors and then down a very rough track that led to one still rougher. 'Suppose we get stuck?' said Diana.

'Then we get stuck,' said James. 'I've got money enough to buy us out of most situations. I know that sounds bloody mercenary but it happens to be true.'

They stopped at last. They were very high up, on a track never used except during the shooting season. Away to the left was a crumbling stone hut, long since abandoned, all around was the circle of wide blue sky.

Stiff heather crunched beneath their feet and a grouse flew up, cackling noisily. James took the rugs from the car and moved to a slight depression in the ground. He laid one rug down. 'The other goes on top,' he explained. 'We don't want to freeze to death.'

Diana smiled. 'No.' She bent and took the hem of her dress in her crossed hands, then peeled it off over her head. James let out his breath in a gasp. Her breasts had begun to sag a little, hanging heavily like oranges in a net. They aroused him unbearably, as her abandon aroused him, the way she spread wide her arms to the wind and the sun. He had not intended to be naked himself until the last minute, had shrunk from the thought of his white body with its scant carrot hair and erotic protuberance exposed to her critical gaze. But to hell with caution, to hell with responsibility, to hell with everything. He ripped off his shirt, dragged off his jeans. He was going to make the most of every sweet, sweat-smelling second.

Andy was playing a gentle, lilting sonata, full of peace and harmony. Diana listened tenderly, her judgment marking the points that required improvement, her senses utterly bewitched. After a while and a couple of jarring passages she stood up and waved him silent. Taking up her own instrument she began to play the same piece, sending the music into every room in the house. Rowan, doing her homework in the kitchen, lifted up her head. Sally left her jigsaw and Andrew, working in the study, felt tears come to his eyes. The playing held everything there was of happiness, and beneath it, whispering, regret.

# Chapter Five

There was an air of bustle about Judge's that Andrew found most heartening. Some of it was the result of the new orders, but there was also the rush of optimism to be taken into account. People who were despairing of Judge's suddenly began to wonder if it might be all right after all, if Mr. Andrew really did have his head screwed on. Weren't they a quality mill, couldn't their work be relied on? Not recently no, I grant you, but it takes a long time to ruin a reputation like Judge's. Let's make a go of it, they said to each other, let's all turn to and make this a success!

It was good to see the men busy, the girls smiling and planning their holidays. It had been a long time since Andrew asked anyone where they were going on holiday because the answer would probably be 'We thought we'd better not this year. We'll wait and see how things turn out.' And, amazingly, he thought it might all be due to James Barton. He must have put in a good word for them, he was the only man with the power to do it. Andrew made a mental note to speak to him at the Textile Dinner later in the week. It was only right that if it had been James Barton, Andrew should show proper gratitude.

Nobby was at his elbow. 'Sorry, Mr. Andrew. Card's gone again. We need a new bearing for the swift.'

Andrew hurried across. The safety guards were swung clear away from the machine and the whole dusty interior was revealed to be nothing more than a procession of spiked rollers, the wool passing from one to the other until it emerged at the end like a transparent carpet and was condensed into a fragile rope of sliver. The main roller, the swift, had been lifted out on a block and tackle.

'See here,' said Nobby. 'You can see what's to do.'

Even Andrew could see the marks of abnormal wear. 'Nobby, we need this card,' he said firmly. 'It'll take too long for a new bearing. It has to run.'

'I'm telling you, Mr. Andrew, it won't.'

'And I'm saying it must!' An inrush of panic made him curt. He tried to sound reasonable. 'Please, Nobby. We cannot afford to deliver this order late. Just get it working, as best you can.'

He turned on his heel and left Nobby looking helplessly at the machine. Andrew's mind raced. What ought he to do? Should he chase the bearing or try and find some other firm to card the wool? Suppose he sent the wool off and then Nobby did get the card to run? Suppose he didn't and the machine stood idle for weeks? Suppose they could after all manage on one card and he was worrying needlessly? All his peace of mind vanished like sunshine in the face of winter.

In his father's day they'd run twenty-four-hour shifts, putting Asians on at night. Nowadays there were no night shifts, and besides, if he ran one exceptionally, the remaining carding machine might crack under the strain. It too was no longer in its first youth. There seemed nothing to do but keep on hoping for the best. Nobby so often fixed things that looked impossible, surely he would do so now?

The Textile Dinner was held in a Bradford hotel, a non-descript place where the food was no more than mediocre and the surroundings uninspired. All the dinners were held there, yet the food never improved and the décor never changed. Like so much else, it had been different in the old days.

Andrew was glad to be out in dinner jacket and bow tie, it avoided another evening of worry. A little socialising might put things in a better perspective, there were sure to be others in a worse mess than himself. Nobby had not repaired the card, and in trying to run it with the bearing gone had sheared a holding pin for another roller. There was a three month wait for the parts, which were out of stock and out of date. After wasting days, Andrew was now trying to find someone who would either card the wool for him, or sell him carded sliver of similar quality. All of it was uncalled for expense and all of it delayed the order. There was no way it could go out on time.

He saw someone he knew, a man who had been at school with him. Rodney Lewis, that was his name, scion of a mohair spinner. 'Hello, Rodney. How are things?'

The other man was florid, running to seed. He was also rather drunk. 'Not so bad, my son. Market's been unstable for so long I'm beginning to get to like it. Got a new machine in though, an absolute bugger. Latest thing and no one knows how to work it. Chewed up stuff all over the shop. Sometimes I wonder why in God's name we don't stick to the old bangers we know and hate.' Delivered of his boasting, Rodney shifted his paunch more comfortably over his trousers and added, 'You through your bad patch, are you? Heard things weren't so good.'

'We're over the worst,' said Andrew quickly. 'I just wish the mill wasn't so old. It's damned hard to run efficiently in a great tomb of a place on five floors. We don't use half of it.'

Rodney nodded sympathetically. Andrew remembered that at school he had been everybody's friend until everybody discovered his little habit of stabbing you in the back. He rushed to put up more of a front. 'We've some very big orders on at the moment. Very big. Thinking about a night shift. Terrible strain for everyone, of course — ' but Rodney had seen someone he liked better, or at least thought could do him more good. He drifted away to drop hints of an imminent Isaac Judge collapse. It might be true, as for so many before.

Andrew had a bad taste in his mouth. He looked around

for a familiar face, but those he saw seemed to be engaged in parties of their own. Then James Barton came in, taller than most, his skin stained with freckles, the carrot hair receding to give him an intellectual look. His dinner suit had the fresh sheen of recent make, noticeable amongst all the let out and retextured models around him. Heads turned to glance surreptitiously, but no one went to speak to him. Andrew seized his chance and bustled across.

'Hello, James. Good to see you. Can I get you a drink?'

For a moment Barton seemed taken aback. A laugh hovered around his mouth. 'Thanks,' he said at last. 'Er — Scotch, I think.'

Andrew caught a waiter and delivered the order. Barton said, 'How's business?' rather quizzically Andrew thought.

'Fine. Just fine. I imagine you put in a good word for me — well, I feel it must have been you. I wanted to thank you. I mean, it's difficult with old machines but I always say it's quality that counts with our market and that we try and achieve —'

Barton cut him off abruptly. 'How's your wife? Have you built her that music room yet?'

They were interrupted by the waiter with the drinks and Andrew paid for them clumsily, counting out silver instead of simply handing over notes.

'Good heavens,' he said as he finished. 'What a memory you must have. We haven't agreed a design yet — it's proving rather dificult. Diana is so particular, you see. I suppose all women are.'

'Yes.' Barton watched him, grey eyes unblinking. 'I hear you're having machinery trouble,' he said suddenly. 'What are you going to do about it?'

His pride stung, Andrew said stiffly, 'I can't imagine why you think it's any concern of yours, James. I assure you everything is under control. I don't have to — I mean it's very kind of you to take such an interest but Judge's has managed very well on its own for a good many years.'

James snorted. 'You really ought to get your finger out. People don't accept late orders these days. They're not interested in your reasons, only your results. Get your business sorted and Diana can have a dozen music rooms!'

'I'm well able to take care of my own wife, thank you,' retorted Andrew. 'And my own business.'

'Glad to hear it. Thanks for the drink.' Barton sauntered off across the room.

Trying to gather his wits, Andrew went out into the foyer. He didn't understand Barton. What made him think he had the right to interfere in Judge's affairs? If one gesture of goodwill meant sacrificing all privacy and independence, then he'd be damned — except, of course, he would be damned. When men like Barton paid the piper, lesser mortals danced.

It was time to go in to dinner. His appetite had fled, he wanted nothing more than to go home and tell Diana about it, to go back into the one safe haven of his home. Instead, he went to his place, made small talk about golf and chewed his way through tough lamb cutlets.

James Barton had indulged himself in attacking Andrew. It was a small revenge for Diana's treatment, for her wilful refusal to need James as much as he needed her. He felt that he had inspired not the least degree of commitment in her, and he was galled that Andrew, so inadequate, should have what he was denied. He had an urge to wreck the neat pattern of Andrew's life, to seize its prizes for himself. In the evenings when he went home to Marjorie and the television, he sat in his airless lounge and thought about Diana.

He took to looking at his wife, assessing her. She was a short woman who had thickened, not excessively but she lacked the height to carry it. And she dressed in dowdy tweeds, neat jumpers, always with a diamond and pearl brooch fastened to the shoulder. No mane of auburn hair for her, but a tidy mid-brown perm. There was nothing vulgar or pretentious about her. She was comfortable with money, sensible with it, living as modestly, sensibly and downright boringly as her mother had done before her. No wonder, she had always been nicely off, and had she not, then James would not have married her. It was a bargain he had kept for many years, fidelity in exchange for hard cash. A bargain he had kept for too long, he now believed. He hadn't known what he was missing. Sometimes James thought he would stifle.

The day after the Textile Dinner he sent Diana a diamond hairclip. The special messenger arrived mid-morning, and as he roared up on his motorbike Diana felt a surge of mingled panic and rage. She knew what was coming. James didn't care if people found out. He wanted them to find out.

She took the box up to her bedroom and opened it well away from the daily's gaze. Her heart turned over. It was an exquisite spray of flowers, perfectly understated. She swept her hair up and tried the clip in it, knowing she could not keep it, that even if she did there would be nowhere it could be worn. Besides, what would Andrew say? She picked up the bedside 'phone.

'Bardsey Textiles? Mr. Barton please. A personal call. Mrs. Judge.'

James came on the line. 'Diana? Darling.'

'James, how dare you? I won't have it. If you do anything like this again then it's all over. I warn you, I won't let you wreck my life. I thought we understood each other.'

'Darling, it's only a present. I can't resist giving you things. I wanted to give you pleasure.'

Diana pressed her fingers to the bony bridge of her nose. 'That's very sweet of you. But you know I couldn't wear it, it's so obviously expensive. Are you trying to trap me, James? Is that it?'

'Look —' he paused and could be heard murmuring to someone in the room — 'darling, I can't talk now. Tomorrow. Please.'

'No.' She replaced the receiver, hard. How dare he talk to her with someone else listening?

Later that day, when the children were home from school, the special messenger roared up to the door once again. He had another package.

'What on earth is it?' demanded Rowan, green eyes sparkling.

'Can I open it? Let me!' squeaked Sally.

Even Andy, who was studying a score, looked up with interest.

'It's probably come to the wrong house,' said Diana desperately. 'I'll take it back tomorrow. It isn't mine.'

'It says you,' said Rowan. 'Anyway, how can you know what it is before you've opened it?'

'Rowan, it's none of your business!' flared Diana. She rushed from the room, the package clutched in her hand. When she opened it, she froze. It was a diamond heart-shaped brooch, and within it were smaller hearts, until in the centre was a large, solitaire diamond. Underneath was a card, and in James's scrawled handwriting she read: 'I love you.'

At dinner, the children were full of the mystery parcel. 'What is it, dear?' asked Andrew curiously.

'A brooch. I think it's for another Mrs. Judge. I certainly don't know anyone likely to send me brooches.'

'Can we see it? Why can't we see it?' Sally bounced up and down, as usual giving her enthusiasm physical expression. When she was happy she bounced, when she was sad she rocked, when she was bored she bit her nails. Stillness, with Sally, probably meant coma.

'I've already wrapped it up to go back,' said Diana firmly. She was only too aware that Andrew was watching her.

When they were alone and drinking coffee, he said, 'Has someone sent you a present?'

Not looking at him, she said, 'There was no name. I really don't know.'

41

'But the children said it was the right address.'

'No, it was just Mrs. Judge.'

'Diana Judge, they said.'

'Really, Andrew, it isn't for me! I shall go to the shop tomorrow and make some enquiries, there's no point in subjecting me to this inquisition. What is it you suspect me of? A clandestine affair?'

'Darling, of course not!' But he looked away.


James drove up at half-past twelve the next day. Diana flung the door open before he reached it. 'How could you! You bastard, get out of here, get away from me!'

James reached out and pushed her back into the hall. She went back hard and hit out at him, bruising her knuckles on his teeth.

'Stop it! Stop it!' He caught her wrist and twisted her arm up behind her back. His lip was bleeding.

'You're hurting. Let me go.' Her eyes were huge, the pupils black with pain. He twisted her arm some more, enjoying it. She cried out and he let go.

'I don't want you any more,' hissed Diana. 'Get out.'

'I won't get out. I love you, and I think you love me. I want us to be together.'

'No, you don't! You just want to win, that's all. You want everything your own way.'

James came close to her, cupping her breasts. 'Why shouldn't I? Why shouldn't you? We're so alike, we want the same things. If I could just see you more often, twice a week, that's all. I don't want to make you unhappy. I want to love you, I *have* to love you!'

When he kissed her she tasted salty blood. When he made love to her on the hard floor it was as violent as a battle.

# Chapter Six

James came to the house on Mondays and Thursdays. Any scruples that Diana felt about betraying her husband in his own house she forced herself to ignore. It was safer here, they were less likely to be seen. James was dangerous, James was prepared to assault her marriage to get what he wanted. Giving in to him, and to her own needs, was the best way out.

People began to say how well she looked, there was a glow about her, a fine shining edge. Odd new items of clothing started appearing. A jacket that Andrew was sure was new but which Diana claimed she had had for ages. A new handbag. And in her handkerchief drawer, found by Andrew and carefully put back, the heart-shaped brooch.

He didn't think about it. He didn't dare think about it. If it was anybody it was James Barton, but of course he was imagining things. They had a life together, they had a family, three wonderful children. But he couldn't help noticing how much less intense she was about Andy's training, how much less short with the girls. If it wasn't for work he would go mad, he knew it. He went to the doctor about loss of appetite.

As for Diana, she was alive! Before James she had been sliding into acid middle-age, years before she was ready for it. It occurred to her that she had been putting too much of herself into Andy's music, because her own music had failed her, through no one's fault but her own. In those valuable years of the late teens Diana had lost her dedication; she had dated and gone to parties, skimping practice and trying to bluff her way through lessons. She had paid for it a thousand times, mourned by her teachers as one of the girls who might have but didn't. Only when it was too late did she regret it, only when she was married to Andrew and the gloss was wearing off. For Diana could have been better than her son, if she had wanted to be. The knowledge gnawed at her soul.

Of course she told herself that with James it was only sex, and in part it was true. They were switched on to each other, they had only to touch to be aroused. Wild, adult sexuality was their own personal discovery, as far from dull marital duty as the earth from the sun. But it was also that, with James, she was herself. There was no need to hold back and be kind, and besides, the enslavement of a man at the top of his particular tree was an achievement which delighted her. She almost wished people knew about it.

Then one day her friend Linda came by for coffee and said excitedly, 'You'll never guess! James Barton's having an affair!'

Diana swallowed. 'How do you know?'

'Well, Gillian is very thick with his wife, Marjorie, and though she doesn't look it − I mean she's a real Mrs. Rabbit, all warm fires and crumpets − she's got her head screwed on. And Marjorie Barton's been finding bills for presents, like diamonds! I thought that went out with the Ark! How I wish someone would send me diamonds.'

Diana's legs felt weak. She knew she should get up and pour more coffee but couldn't. 'Well, the woman can't be married then,' she said desperately. 'A married woman couldn't have diamonds, her husband would notice.'

Linda wrinkled her nose. 'If it was me, I'd keep them and hide them. Then I could drool over them in my old age, and remember when I was being screwed by a rich old man!'

'James Barton isn't old!' snapped Diana.

'Not really, no. I quite fancy him actually,' added Linda thoughtfully. 'He's got that wonderful streak of cruelty − you just know he's the sort that enjoys squashing flies. Probably got some woman he can tie to the bed and flog. If

44

you did that to Marjorie Barton she'd witter away about the best type of whip and don't mark the wallpaper.'

Diana laughed. It amazed her how much she liked to hear James's wife being slated.

The next afternoon she let James take her to bed straight away, something she didn't usually permit. She liked him to suffer. As he reached out for her, she caught hold of his erection and gripped hard.

'Your wife knows about us.'

He grunted. She looked for the expression of alarm, but there was none. He flexed against her hand. 'You want her to know,' she whispered.

In answer James ducked his head and fastened his teeth on her breast, biting hard and leaving a clear crescent, like a brand. Diana shrieked and tried to get free of him, but he pushed her down and somehow, in the struggle, got inside. They lay together, staring and angry.

'This is the end,' said Diana. 'I won't leave Andrew.'

'He'll kick you out when he knows,' said James.

'Will he?' She laughed up at him, in control even now. 'I'll tell him I was mad, I'll tell him I'm sorry. He'll forgive me.'

'God, but you think you're so clever!' He bucked into her and she gasped; he knew that he was exciting her, that soon she would be satisfied. And he couldn't bring himself really to hurt her. 'I love you, Diana!' he panted, watching the sweat form in the hollow of her throat, seeing her eyes close to exclude him. He would never let her go!

Nothing more was said about ending it. But the next Thursday, when James called, she was out. There was a letter lying on the step.

Dear James,

I meant what I said. If you really want to hurt me, then I suppose you will tell Andrew, but you'll gain nothing by it. I don't like being threatened. Please don't try and get

in touch with me, because I think we both know we
should stop now, before we get ourselves in a real mess.
Don't think I'm not grateful for what we've had. You are
a very remarkable person.

Love, Diana

He started to laugh. The letter seemed to epitomise all that
she did not know about him. The depth of her ignorance, in
thinking that she could so easily just stop when it pleased
her, was a challenge. It was time she learned what had got
him where he was today, time she saw some part of the
tenacity that had dragged a tired firm to the pinnacle of
success. The battle to come delighted him, he was grateful to
her for adding this twist to the story. At the same time,
denied her, he wanted her more than ever. It seemed nothing
could make up for what he could not now have.

He slammed back into his car, seeing a child's bicycle
lying by the path to the front door. Quickly he turned the
Mercedes and crushed it under his wheels.

In the evening Sally was in tears over her bicycle. 'I'm sure
we'll get you a new one,' said Diana distractedly. 'Just stop
making such a fuss, Sally!' She was trying to listen to Andy
practise, and Rowan had the television turned up again, and
she had a splitting headache and a feeling as if her skin was
being attacked by insects. He might have gone straight
round to Andrew, in which case this evening's chaos could
only get worse.

But when Andrew came in he seemed much as usual. He
flared when he heard about the bicycle though. 'Sally, it's
entirely your own fault, you left the blasted thing there! We
can't afford a new one, there's no question of it. Diana, why
didn't you make her put it away? Who was it anyway?'

'How should I know, I was out,' shrieked Diana. 'God,
Rowan, will you turn off that damned television!'

Andrew went stonily upstairs to get changed, and

afterwards everyone sat down to supper. It was soon clear that Andrew had no appetite.

'Is something the matter?' Diana forced herself to ask the question.

Andrew cleared his throat. 'Not really. Well, yes. The new order's been cancelled. It should have been going out next week and we were going to be late, but it seems they heard and cancelled it.'

'Couldn't you do a deal?' demanded Diana. 'You can pay a forfeit, can't you?'

'I did suggest it, yes. They wouldn't listen.'

Into the silence piped Sally's voice. 'I can't have a new bike, then?'

'Shut up, Sally,' said Rowan. She was staring at her father out of intense green eyes. 'We're not finished, are we?'

He tried to smile. 'Of course not, darling.'

Andy, as usual self-absorbed, said, 'I've been asked to do three pieces for the school concert. But I'll only do two, I don't want to practise lollipop music all the time.'

'Just about your level,' snapped Rowan. 'Can't you see this is important?'

'And it's nothing to do with you,' rebuked Diana. 'Honestly, Andrew, why do you have to worry the children? That firm is always in trouble: if it isn't late orders It's wrong dyes or faults in the weave or poor quality or something! Why can't you for once get to grips with it?'

The outburst surprised even her. Andrew said, 'It may well be my fault. I do my best, that's all I can say.'

'Of course you do,' said Diana frostily. 'I'm sorry.'

In the bedroom that night, he said, 'I am sorry, you know.'

'What about?' Diana was distracted, hoping very much that he would not want to make love to her, because her breast was still so bruised.

'About making such a mess of things. I know I'm not making you happy.'

She couldn't meet his eyes. Yet at the same time she hated him for making her feel so terribly, damnably guilty! If he was more like James, she found herself thinking, if he fought back instead of meekly going under, then there would be no need to apologise. James was striking at Andrew, and at her, and it was what she would have done in his place.

'I am happy,' she said distantly.

'Diana — are you sure? It's just I've wondered — I mean, you're an attractive woman, a beautiful woman. I wouldn't be surprised if —'

As he tailed off, Diana's mind raced. Had James told him or was he guessing? Trust Andrew to beat about the bush in this cowardly way!

'I don't know what you're talking about, Andrew,' she announced, flinging back the sheets and getting into bed. 'Stop worrying about me and get on with running the firm. If you've lost this order you can get others, but no one's going to do if for you!'

She lay down and determinedly turned off her bedside light, her position in the bed making it clear that she did not want him to touch her. Andrew knew he wouldn't be able to sleep, the thoughts were buzzing in his head. Why had the order been cancelled like that? A brief message to say they had been informed by Bardsey that the delivery was likely to be late, and that Bardsey were arranging for the order to be fulfilled from elsewhere. What in God's name did it have to do with Bardsey, and why had they given the order in the first place, only to take it away now? Was it a plot to destroy him? Did it have everything to do with Diana or nothing at all?

He lay down and closed his eyes, trying to calm himself. He was almost crying. Suddenly, painfully, he longed for his father, he wanted to cry out to him for help and guidance, the unfailing wisdom that had been his prop for so long. But he was quite, quite alone.

# Chapter Seven

The Summer Ball was an event the Judges seldom missed, and now with rumours flying they were compelled to go. The Bartons did not normally attend, but for some reason this year James told his wife that they would. And attend they did, he immaculate in his dinner jacket, she frumpy in an expensive but unsuitable tulle frock. James and Majorie were standing together when the Judges entered. Diana was wearing tawny shot taffeta, long-sleeved, high-necked and infinitely seductive. Marjorie Barton felt the electricity in her husband, it leaped the space between them. 'So,' she thought, 'that's her.'

James took hold of his wife's arm and bore her across to be introduced. Andrew's face turned to stone but Diana's cool never faltered.

'Good heavens, Mr. Barton,' she said lightly.

'How nice to see you, Mrs. Judge. Andrew. May I introduce my wife, Marjorie?'

They were polite to each other. Andrew was intent on moving away, the very presence of Barton made him feel shaky. But James would have none of it. Working with absolute determination he insisted they all go to the same table, ordered champagne, chatted as if they were all firm friends. The band was playing a quickstep.

'Do you dance, Diana?' said James. 'Come on, Andrew, let's show the ladies a good time.' He took hold of Diana's arm, a determined clasp. She could have resisted, she almost did, but when she saw his roguish smile it was matched with her own. 'All right,' she said and stood up. Andrew and Marjorie were left looking at one another.

On the floor James said, 'Thanks for the letter.'

'Bastard,' said Diana dispassionately. 'We're nearly ruined.'

'Oh no, I give you at least three months. I should have done for you by then, I think.'

She looked him full in the face. 'What does it take to make you stop? Do you want me to sleep with you again?'

He grinned, like a wolf with an empty belly. 'That was what the price used to be. But it's gone up. If you leave him and come to me, he can keep his business. I'll pull out all the stops for him, help him all the way. If you stay, then it goes down.'

She gasped. 'You're not serious!'

'Absolutely. Have you missed me, Diana?'

'No.' But they both knew it wasn't true. They were dancing very close, and it was as much her doing as his. He could feel her trembling.

She put her lips to his ear. 'Please, James, don't be so cruel. I've my children to think of. Please, can't it be like it was?'

Andrew and Marjorie danced by. Two anxious faces watching them. James murmured, 'I'm going to marry you,' almost loud enough for them to hear. And suddenly he meant it. He danced Diana to the open floor-length window, and pushed her out on to the terrace. Below stretched the gardens, dark and mysterious. He caught Diana's hand and pulled her down the steps and across the damp grass. Hidden in the shadow of a tree he began to kiss her. 'Say you love me! Say it!'

'I love you! I love you!' She responded wildly, tasting the skin of his face, the sting of aftershave, the dregs of his champagne. At least here, in these few moments, she could let go, have an end to the tensions of home, the unspoken accusations, the failures. This man matched and exceeded her. She didn't have to be kind for he wasn't kind, any more than she.

In the ballroom, Marjorie clutched at Andrew's arm. 'They've gone outside. I wonder why.'

'It is hot in here,' said Andrew, looking like an ostrich as he watched the hem of his wife's dress slip out of sight.

'But you know what's been going on, don't you?' She stared up at him, plain, frightened, someone he didn't know who wanted to talk about things he dared not think of.

'Going on? I'm sure it isn't − I trust my wife. Of course I do − ' His feet faltered in the rhythm of the dance and he crushed Marjorie's toes, but she didn't seem to notice.

'If we go, then we'll know, won't we? I've got to know.' She pulled insistently at his arm and reluctantly he went with her, although he didn't want to know, could not bear to know.

It was dark in the garden, and with relief he thought they wouldn't find them. But Marjorie, in sensible shoes, hurried unerringly across the grass. And in the darkness, there was the gleam of shot taffeta, the animal sounds of people locked in passion. Let her not be naked, prayed Andrew. Spare me that. But still, when he saw her neck stretched back for James to mouth the skin, the neck that she had passed on to Rowan and which drooped so diffidently in their daughter, he thought he would be sick. He let out a cry, like a creature gripped in a snare. They froze. Their heads turned towards him.

Andrew was sobbing, open-mouthed. 'Why? Why did you have to?'

Diana tried to move out of James's arms, but he held on. Andrew embarrassed her, she wished he would control himself. Why was it that he never ever responded to crisis in a way that impressed her? 'I'm sorry, Andrew,' she said grittily. 'I didn't mean you to know.'

'But you did, didn't you, James,' said Marjorie bitterly. 'That's why I'm here, to be shown, isn't it? Well, I've decided. I'm not going to put up with you. I'm not going to let you humiliate me. You can have what you bloody well like, but I'm not going to give up my house or one single thing in it.'

James laughed. He was enjoying every minute of this, because he had constructed the scene, and he was the one coming out best. 'Well done, Marjorie,' he said cheerfully. 'I always did like your good sense, if very little else. You never keep on with a losing streak, I suppose you learned that from your father, unlike Andrew here. He never seems to know when to quit.'

'You bastard!' Andrew launched himself at James, fingers clawed. In one continuous movement James put Diana to one side, ducked and hit Andrew in the balls. He fell in motionless agony.

'Oh my God,' moaned Diana, and knelt at his side, her hair in her eyes. 'Andrew, I'm sorry, I'm sorry. Let's go home, Andrew. I won't leave you, I promise, let's go home.' Then looking up at James she screamed, 'Why did you have to hurt him? I hate you!'

Marjorie snorted and said, 'It's a fine time to find that out. Oh, you go to him, Mrs. Judge, and see how long it is before he's bored with you.'

A crowd was gathering, and James decided that enough was enough. He gestured to Marjorie. 'Go to the car. I'll drive you home, then I'll go to the club. Diana, let's get Andrew up, you'd better take him home.'

'Don't touch him,' sobbed Diana, but obediently took one arm while James took the other. People parted to let them stagger through, Andrew coughing with pain.

They put him in the back and then Diana flung herself behind the wheel. James caught the door and held it open. 'I'll come round tomorrow. I won't let it go on, I know what it's like for you.'

'It isn't going to happen, James.' She glared up at him, and they both knew she didn't mean it, that they weren't turning back, either of them. He bent his head and kissed her, knowing that he had won. He felt a massive upsurge of exhilaration.

Diana drove away fast. By the time they reached home Andrew could speak, but he wasn't speaking, he was crying. 'Please, Andrew, stop it,' begged Diana. 'I didn't want it to be, like this!' She got him out of the car and pushed him towards the house. 'We'll talk about it later, tomorrow, we'll feel better then.'

'Tomorrow!' he shrieked. 'You won't even be here tomorrow! Is it the money, is it that? What do you want, Diana, what do you want me to give you?'

Rowan appeared at the top of the stairs. 'Mummy? What's the matter?'

Diana tried to pull herself together. Andrew was ranting at the top of his voice. 'Nothing, darling. Daddy's not well.'

He rushed up the stairs towards Rowan. 'That's right, yes, I'm not well. I can't stomach the sight of her and her lover. Your mother's been fucking another man, how do you like that, Rowan? Even tonight, there they were, pawing each other! Where did you do it, Diana? In the car, in his big flash car, or in some sleazy motel?'

'In our bed, actually,' said Diana. It was an impulse of cruelty she was beyond repressing. 'Go to bed, Rowan.'

The girl's shocked face retreated. Andrew seized hold of Diana's shoulders and shook her, shouting: 'Bitch! Prostitute! If you don't care about me, then what about them? All right, go to him, leave us all and go, I don't want you here!' But then he let her go. He couldn't bear it if she left him.

In the end he slept on the sofa, and Diana went upstairs. All the children were awake, woken by the smashing of plates and the screaming. Diana had a swelling bruise on the side of her face but she was controlled.

'Is it true?' demanded Rowan, fierce in a white nightie. She had her arm around Sally, who was very frightened.

'Of course it isn't,' said Andy. 'Dad's drunk.'

'I'll explain in the morning,' said Diana. 'You must all go to bed.'

'It is true then,' said Rowan. 'It's the man that sent you the brooch.'

Diana paused. At that instant she deeply disliked her eldest child, who at fifteen sat there and judged her with as little sympathy as a lump of marble. 'You can think what you like, Rowan,' she said stiffly. 'If you want to think that I would do things I should be ashamed of, then you may.'

'Of course you wouldn't do anything bad,' declared Andy loyally. 'It's the firm, that's the trouble.'

Diana smiled at him, tapping the deep well of her love for her son. 'That's right, Andy. Mostly it's because of the firm.'

At dawn Andrew could be heard downstairs, definitely drunk this time, and breaking things with a hammer. Diana remained behind closed doors, so Rowan went down. She stood and watched her father breaking a china cabinet, smashing the little cups and figurines with drunken precision.

'Please don't, Daddy,' she said tremulously. He turned and saw her, and his face crumpled.

'She doesn't love me any more,' he said mournfully. 'She loves him. She's going to leave us and go to him.'

'Would you like a hanky?' asked Rowan. She held out a tissue and Andrew took it, mopping his streaming face. 'We still love you,' said Rowan. Her father's face twisted again, he fought against grief and gave in to it. Rowan put out her arms and held him.

It was a week before Diana left, a week of horrors. In every hour Andrew swung from rage to wild grief; from begging her to stay to threatening to throw her out, then and there. If James Barton appeared he threatened to knife him and once Rowan, who had not dared go to school, stood in the kitchen with her back to the door to prevent her father from going out and stabbing both James and Diana. In the end he slashed the door inches above her head, while she stood too terrified even to close her eyes. And afterwards, awash with guilt, he talked about killing himself.

'I've got to go,' Diana said to her, in an attempt at explanation. 'He'll be better once I've gone, he'll come to terms with it. I never thought he'd take it so hard.'

'Why don't you say you're sorry? He'd make up. You know he can't stay cross for long.'

'I'm afraid I can't,' said Diana. 'James — Mr. Barton — he has a lot of power. I don't think the firm would survive if he didn't — if I didn't.'

'Daddy would still rather you stayed,' said Rowan implacably.

Diana struggled for honesty. 'Perhaps I don't want to stay. I think we've both changed, your father and me. We don't seem to know each other very well. Or we might know each other too well, I don't really understand it. I — need — somebody like Mr. Barton.'

'I won't live with him,' said Rowan.

'Well —' Diana had not even considered this possibility. But now she did she put forward the conventional solution. 'Of course, when we're settled you will, and see Daddy at weekends. The children always go with the mother.'

'Well, I won't,' said Rowan. 'And I'll tell Sally not to either.'

'God, Rowan, you can be a little beast!' snarled her mother, and slapped her, hard, on the leg.

When James came finally to take Diana, Rowan tried to keep her father away. But he stormed out of the house, unshaven, his clothes a mess, raving like a maniac. James feared him not at all. 'What in God's name do you think you look like?' he said.

Andrew stood there, shaking, unable even to frame a coherent response. He rubbed his hand against his face, saying confusedly, 'You mustn't take her. You can't.'

Rowan ran out of the house, prepared to do battle where her father would not. There had to be something she could do to stop this, there had to be some way of putting it right. James Barton stared at her calmly. She wanted to kill him. She stood before him, fists clenched, and screamed: 'You're spoiling our home! It's your fault we're all so sad, we all hate you. We'll hate you forever.' The words weren't enough, but she had nothing else. If she had a gun she would shoot him and her mother, dent that terrible, calm control.

'Will you now?' For once James was slightly nonplussed. She was so boyishly tall, and so clearly enraged. 'You'll feel better when things have settled down,' he managed.

'I am never going into a house with you in it,' sneered Rowan. 'I would choke to breathe the same air. You're disgusting, ugly and old and perverted. Both of you are.' She included her mother in a searing glance of contempt.

'Rowan! At least you can be polite,' snapped Diana. 'I'm sorry, James, she's upset. I should have made sure she went to school with Sally and Andy.'

'Then who would take care of Dad?' demanded Rowan. 'You don't care about him at all, all you care about is you, you, you!'

'Don't go away,' begged Andrew. 'Diana, my darling, you know how I love you!'

'No, you don't,' screamed Rowan in a voice that sounded years too young for her. 'You hate her, we all do! Daddy, don't talk like that in front of *him*!'

Andrew slumped on to the low wall that bordered the drive. He dropped his head into his hands and wailed.

'Daddy! Daddy, don't!' hissed his daughter.

'Goodbye,' said Diana. 'I'll be in touch.' She got into the car. James got in too, but on a sudden impulse leaned out of the window to wink triumphantly full in the face of Rowan's rage.

She threw stones as the car drove away, but they all missed. 'Oh God,' said Andrew. 'Oh God, I want to die.'

'We should be glad she's gone,' declared Rowan. 'She's horrible. We don't want her here.'

Wrung out with emotion, Andrew said dully: 'It was all my fault, you see. I failed her so terribly.'

'Of course you didn't!' Although he seemed not to listen to anything she said, Rowan tried to bolster him. She was hoarse with screaming, her throat hurt. She coughed and said bitterly, 'She's the real failure. She hasn't done anything herself, but she wants other people to do things. And she's wicked, she'll go to hell and burn and I wish she was there now. I hate her!'

Andrew sighed, again close to tears. 'I don't. Oh, Rowan, how are we to manage without her?' He looked about him at the lovely old house, the garden in full summer bloom, and it seemed to him that he was faced with a barren moonscape, without any of the essentials for life. He couldn't think of any way of going on.

# Chapter Eight

Rowan sat in the windowseat and bit her nails. Andy was practising again, endless runs of scales, oblivious to the anguish around him. Rowan hated the sound of the violin; in a moment she would go and hit him till he stopped.

It was three weeks since Diana had left, and Andrew had hardly been out of the house once. Sometimes someone from the mill telephoned, but he wouldn't talk to them. Today Rowan's form mistress had called and Rowan had lied, saying she had been ill with 'flu and would be back next week. She hadn't dared let Miss Perkins see Andrew; she'd send him to a mental home and put all three children into care.

Sally wandered in, the collar of her school blouse black with dirt. 'What are we going to eat, Rowan?'

'There isn't anything. And there isn't any money.'

Sally watched her with huge eyes. 'Then what are we going to do?'

And that indeed was the question Rowan had been pondering for hours. Where did money come from? How did you eat when you didn't have any? For as long as she could remember they had been poor, in so far as they didn't have a Porsche or foreign holidays, but they went to private schools and had tennis lessons. No money for food was more than poor, it was destitute.

'Why don't we ask Mummy?' said Sally.

'No! And don't you dare try and get in touch with her, I'd rather we all died.' Every time Diana 'phoned, Rowan made sure she answered and hung up as soon as she realised who it was. Because it was no use pretending she cared now; if she

59

had really cared she wouldn't have gone.

Sally sat down on the carpet and started making a jigsaw with some of the broken pieces of china that still lay there, not cleared away. The daily had abandoned them in the first week, she wouldn't work for nothing. 'I wish Daddy would get up,' said Sally mournfully.

Rowan unwound her long legs from the window seat. She went slowly upstairs to the spare room, where her father now slept because he would not lie down in a bed 'Where your mother fornicated with that bastard!' as he kept on saying. When she knocked on the door, there was no response, so she turned the handle and went in.

Andrew was lying on top of the bed, staring blindly at the ceiling. He had lain like that for days and days, stirring only to go to the bathroom and occasionally to eat what Rowan provided for him. 'Daddy,' she said anxiously, 'we haven't any money.'

His head turned. 'We never have any money.'

'But — we can't buy food. I don't know what to do.'

His face quivered. 'And now you're hungry. Now my children are going hungry! Oh God, I can't bear it.' He put his hands over his face and Rowan suppressed an urge to hit him. Why wouldn't he get up and do something, instead of lying there not bearing it? If he didn't, who would?

She left him and went back downstairs. Money, they had to have money. The place to get money was the bank, and she would go there tomorrow and see how you got some. For tonight she might be able to steal some food perhaps — though she didn't think she'd be very good at it and would probably get caught. Borrowing, then. Humiliating as it would certainly be, she would have to ask someone if she could borrow some money.

Briefly she considered asking the neighbours, but they lived as the Judges did, in the isolation of their acres of gardens, and they didn't know them well. Besides, such people wouldn't just lend you five pounds. They would call down officialdom in all its horrible forms and the children would certainly end up in care. Rowan went into the utility room and put on her scuffed trainers. She had long, thin feet that she felt to be unfemininely large, and she often went around barefoot because they seemed more attractive that way. They didn't look so big somehow, and the long toes might have been elegant. The violin scales still persisted, so she called out to Sally, 'I'm just going out, Sal. I'll be back with some shopping.'

She had no money for the bus, so she had a long walk to the mill, and no time to waste if she was to be there before it closed. Rowan wasn't sure what time it did close, perhaps seven? Someone was sure to be there who would help her. They would have money to give her. But when, at last, she trudged wearily down the narrow street, the gates to Isaac Judge were closed.

She refused to believe she had come all this way for nothing. If she could get into the mill, then she could take a typewriter or something and sell it. After all, it was her father's firm, it was all theirs really. She went round to the little side gate that the watchman used, and to her relief it was unlocked, and so too was the side door into the mill itself. But in the cavernous, echoing interior she was engulfed by a wave of loneliness and fear. Hunger made her weak. She would have liked to curl up on the hard stone floor and give up the struggle, but here, in the ghostly mill, she dared not.

Water was dripping somewhere, an eerie, echoing sound, and in the half light every shadow might have been a monster. When she was little Rowan had had nightmares about wolves eating her, and even now shadows made her heart stutter. If she could get to her father's office there would at least be familiar things to comfort her.

Somehow, alone, she couldn't quite work out where she was in the mill. When she came here with her father she simply followed him around, she didn't navigate for herself.

So in the twilight she blundered into the dye-house and soaked her feet in the orange puddles on the floor, then she trailed her orange footsteps through into the weaving shed. It was unnaturally quiet, when always before there had been the clatter of looms. But then she had never been in the mill when it wasn't working. As she tried to find the door to the offices, she couldn't help noticing how few looms were actually in use, and perhaps more significantly, how few of the great wooden balloons, on which the warp threads of each piece of cloth were laboriously set out prior to weaving, had anything on them at all.

Real fear touched her. Suppose the firm went under and her father hadn't even that to keep him going? All her life Isaac Judge had been a name that filled her with a sense of security, of times past leading on to times to come. The difficulties had always been there, but it was understood that things would pick up, as so many times before. Now, when everything else was crumbling, it was unthinkable that this should go as well. Fate couldn't let it happen all at once.

Her eye lighted on the narrow door that led up to her father's office and she slipped through it thankfully. The stone back stairs led directly into the main corridor, and received ten times more wear than the posh wooden staircase because of the continual dashing up and down to see how things were going where it counted, in the mill. That was the way things had always been: keep an eye on the product and the selling will do itself.

Just as she reached out to open the door of her father's office, Rowan froze. There was a noise. Someone – something – was inside. Her impulse was to turn and run, as fast as she could, away and out. But who could it be in there? It was her father's office, no one had any right! Reaching out with terrified determination, she pushed open the door and confronted – the cleaner, Elsie, who had been at Judge's forever.

'Hello, Rowan love. How are you?' Elsie's squinting

gaze focused on her kindly. Rowan, faced with the impossibility of making a suitable reply, twisted her hands together.

'Heard your dad wasn't well,' said Elsie diplomatically. She knew, as did all Bradford, that Diana Judge had done a flit with James Barton, and they were even now set up in luxury in the Midland Hotel, buying a bottle of champagne every night and getting up to no good at all in a four-poster bed. But it wasn't something to talk about with the daughter, who was only fifteen and a beanpole that blushed. 'Fancy a cup of tea?' added Elsie. 'I always make one about this time. Breaks the night up.'

'Thanks.'

They went off to the little kitchen that served the offices, and Elsie brewed tea and added condensed milk. Rowan almost gagged on it, because she was so terribly hungry. She had eaten nothing all day. 'You all right, love?' asked Elsie. It was hard to tell if she was looking intently at you or not, because her squint made it seem as if she could be staring at a point over your left shoulder.

Rowan took a deep breath. 'I wondered, Elsie – I know this must seem a bit odd – but, well, I'm in a bit of trouble.'

'Oh, yes?' said Elsie cautiously, because her own daughter's trouble was now two years old and a right handful. 'What sort of trouble?'

Rowan looked her more or less in the eyes. 'I haven't got any money. And I need some because there isn't anything to eat, and my sister's only ten and she didn't eat her school lunch today, because it was liver. Andy ate his, but he's thirteen and he gets awfully hungry. I mean, it's only for tonight really because tomorrow I'll go and see the bank manager and he'll give me some money, but for now – well. I haven't any.'

Elsie did not show the least sign of surprise. 'Where's your dad then?' she asked.

'At home, in bed. He's not well. I can't – he doesn't – I

don't think he understands.'

Elsie, who did understand, asked no further questions. She reached for her handbag, a dusty brown affair crammed with papers. In a plastic bag at the back she kept her Christmas savings, four ten-pound notes at this time of year. She took them all and gave them to Rowan.

'I'm sure I don't need that much,' said Rowan in embarrassment. 'I will pay you back, I promise.'

'Let's not talk about that now,' said Elsie firmly. 'But you'll have to speak to your mother and get something sorted out. This is no way for children to live, no way at all. I've known your father a long time, and he isn't a man who can cope, he never has been. It's for your mother to see to you.'

'I am never going to talk to her again,' said Rowan, and she looked so fierce that Elsie paused in her homily.

'Well, that's as may be, but she's the one with the money now, and you children need it. I'll tell you something. One of my lads works here in the finishing, and he says the place is on its knees. Matter of weeks he says, the secretary doesn't even know where the wages is to come from. So your dad can't help you, only your mum. And if it isn't either of them, then it'll be the social, and that's not what you're used to, I'm sure!'

Rowan pushed the money into the pocket of her jeans. One of the first rules she had ever learned was never to talk the firm down. 'I'm sure he's wrong,' she recited automatically. 'My father will soon be back at work, putting everything in order. And of course I'll pay you back, Elsie, I really do promise. Thank you so much.'

She trudged home, half-dead with weariness. The fish and chip shop was open, and she ordered four lots of haddock and chips, knowing that they would be lukewarm by the time she walked home. And when she got there Andrew didn't want his and Andy gobbled it, complaining that he would have preferred a pie.

'Why don't you help? All you do is play that beastly violin!' flared Rowan.

'That's because I have to. It doesn't mean I don't care.' Andy's eyes, so like his mother's, stared at her. Then he said, 'By the way, I put the washing in the machine, all the shirts and blouses and things. If we don't go to school looking decent, people will know.'

'They know anyway,' said Sally. 'They just stop talking about it when I come in.'

'I hate Mummy,' said Rowan shakily. 'It's all her fault.'

'It's that man,' said Andy. 'They should put him in prison with rats.'

Without saying anything, Sally began to cry.

In the morning Rowan went out early and bought bread and cereal from a little shop run by an Asian who survived by being open forever. The shop always smelled strange and usually she only ever bought sweets there. Now, standing in the early morning queue of people buying cigarettes, she felt conspicuous and pushed the money over defiantly. It seemed to be going so fast, and it was all she had.

The post brought a final demand from the electricity board, but she said nothing to anyone and hid it behind the clock. Once Andy and Sally had left on the school bus, she tried to gather her courage. Dad's bank was in Bradford, so she would have to go in on the bus, dressed up in the horrible suit Diana had bought her for Christmas. The sleeves were two inches too short by now but it would have to do, she couldn't wear her favourite jeans and Sitting Bull T-shirt. And she would have to look older than she was.

Her few experiments with make-up had brought derision from her schoolfriends as well as her brother, so she normally didn't wear any. Now, though, she struggled with mascara, avoiding the eye-shadow that always seemed to be her downfall. Colours looked garish on her, because her eyes were so very green. Just at the tricky bit, the telephone rang. It was Diana.

'Rowan! Please, please don't hang up. How is everyone?'

'I don't know why you bother to ask.'

'Because I care about you. Darling, how are you managing? Why aren't you at school, I thought your father would answer.'

'I've got a cold,' lied Rowan.

'Oh dear. Is Andy all right? And Sally?'

'They're at school,' said Rowan non-committally.

'That's good, I am glad. Darling, James and I have been talking. We're moving into a new house at the end of the month ... actually it's an old house, very old, with wonderful gardens and a trout pond with a fountain. You children will absolutely love it. You can have your rooms done just exactly as you like, and there's a turret room with a clock —'

'I'm not coming. I'm staying here.'

Diana's almost panicky recital stopped. 'I wish you wouldn't hate me,' she said.

'And we wish you hadn't gone. I can't talk now, I'm busy.' She put the 'phone down and then viciously ripped up the telephone notepad, throwing the pieces on the floor to add to the general mire of neglect. She went up to see her father.

The room smelled stale and dirty. Andrew was sitting up, reading through old letters. 'That was her,' said Rowan.

'Did she ask about me? What did she say?'

'She wants me and Andy and Sal to go and live with her,' said Rowan, and watched her father's face.

It dropped just a little more. 'I suppose that's generally the way things go, isn't it?' he murmured.

'Well, I won't go!' declared his daughter. 'But, Daddy, what's going to happen? You ought to be at work, you can't stay home forever!'

'Why not? I tried my best with Judge's and I couldn't get

66

it right. Perhaps things will be better if I don't try at all. I don't know what else to do, Rowan, I don't know the answers.'

'We've got to do something. How are we going to live?'

He seemed to be giving it some thought. Then, without warning, he picked up a letter and said, 'You know, she used to like me. See what she says here. "I loved you last weekend, you were wonderful." I mean, she felt that once, it wasn't a lie.'

Rowan sighed. She couldn't expect her father to help her.

When she arrived at the bank she didn't know who to ask for, and consequently they kept her standing at the Enquiry desk for ten minutes while the staff cast curious glances in her direction. She could feel the gossip flying about her like winged insects. At last they took her upstairs and into the presence of a large, craggy man in a battered suit.

'My name's Blood,' he said jovially. 'A pretty dreadful name but there it is. And you are Miss Judge, I understand?'

'I'm Rowan Judge, yes.' She was tense and unsmiling, miserable in the outgrown suit and unglamorous flat shoes, chosen to make her feel shorter. She sat down before the desk and they eyed each other. He was going to try and put her at ease, she knew, making little jokes and so on, and she couldn't bear it.

'I've come to ask for money,' she burst out. 'My mother's left home, my father's having some sort of breakdown and the business is going to collapse. So I need some money. Please.'

Mr. Blood blinked. He had seen some customers in his time, but they weren't usually quite so tall, so pale or so desperate. He had the feeling that one word out of place would cause all that brittle control to snap into pieces. 'Why exactly do you want the money?' he asked cautiously.

'To live, of course!' said Rowan. 'To buy food and pay the bills — since my mother left it's been nothing but bills —

and they're going to turn off the electricity next week. I mean, I know you're not a charity but this is where Dad has his account, isn't it? There is money in it?'

Mr. Blood grunted, as if at a blow in the solar plexus. The one thing the Judge account never had in it was money. It was full of anguish, hopes, promises and despair, but not money. The Judge family had been living on overdraft for so long that he had ceased to look for a day when they were in credit. And the worst of it was, if things were as bad as the girl said, she was going to have to lose her home as well, to at least in part pay the debt.

'I really shouldn't talk about the family's affairs with you at all,' he prevaricated.

'Well, there isn't anyone else,' said Rowan. 'And I'm the one that needs the money.'

'Yes. Yes, I can see your point. How old are you?'

'Seventeen,' she lied, knowing that at her height no one ever knew her age. Eighteen would have been better, but she didn't think she'd get away with it.

The answer seemed to satisfy Mr. Blood because he rang through for the Isaac Judge file. While it came, they sat and stared at each other, Mr. Blood trying to make conversation and Rowan saying nothing. At last the file arrived and Mr. Blood said jovially, 'Well now, let's see if we can explain a thing or two, shall we?' reminding Rowan somehow of visits to Father Christmas, when you came out of the grotto clutching a disappointingly cheap plastic doll. She tried to concentrate on what he was saying, because he was trying to explain the firm's entanglements and it was not easy to understand.

'Is it all Dad's fault?' she asked suddenly.

Mr. Blood paused. 'It isn't easy running a business. It's the hardest thing there is.'

Rowan's clear green gaze remained fixed on the columns of figures he drew for her, because at least no one could pretend things about sums, they were as they were and deceived no one. 'This is the limit of the mill's credit,' explained Mr. Blood. 'Now, unless someone pays in some money next week, we shan't be able to let anyone at Judge's have the money to pay the wages. You can see that, can't you?'

'Yes. But if we don't pay the wages I can have some for us to live on, can't I? I could have some now.'

'Well — you could,' said Mr. Blood carefully. 'But then the firm would be out of business and there would be no way of paying off this overdraft. We should have to sell your house.'

'Is it worth all this?' demanded Rowan.

'No. We should still be owed an awful lot of money. We should have to sell the mill, the stock, the machinery, everything.'

'Oh.'

Rowan sat peering down at the figures. Mr. Blood reflected on what a strange-looking girl she was, with her long thin extremities, her small, short-haired head on a long thin neck. What a pity her clothes didn't fit her. Rowan said, 'I'd better just have fifty pounds, I think. I've got to talk to my father. We have to get some money in. He's always talking about people who owe him money.'

Mr. Blood looked pained. For how long had he too been talking to Andrew Judge about the people who owed money, begging him to get tough. At least his daughter realised the urgency. 'Can you do that, do you think?' he asked.

'I don't know,' she said. 'I can have the fifty pounds, though, can't I?'

'Oh yes,' said Mr. Blood. 'I think you deserve it.'

Rowan felt calmer on the way home. When you faced problems, when you knew what it was that was frightening you, although you still felt scared, you weren't paralysed any more. If, when all her money was gone, they were still in

69

this mess, then she would go to her mother and ask for help, if not for her then for Sally and Andy. But until then she had a breathing space in which to try, and it was worth it because being paid for by James Barton would choke her. She passed a hamburger place and bought herself the cheapest take-away. The electricity board would have to be staved off; she would ring them up and say they'd already paid, it would take a while to sort out. Eventually no doubt the telephone would be cut off, and the gas and everything. And even after the hamburger she was still hungry.

When she got home, Andrew was sleeping. She stood looking down at him, wondering why he looked so much more handsome when asleep. There was none of the anxious hesitation of his waking hours, just a clear, calm face. She was overwhelmed with protective love for him.

'Dad. Dad, please wake up.'

He did so slowly, recollection of his whereabouts, his situation, sweeping back into him. Wrinkles formed on his brow. 'What is it?'

'Dad, I've been to see the bank. You've got to get dressed now and go back to work, it's really important. We don't have to worry about orders or anything, we've got to get the money that's owed. I'll come with you, I'll help.'

'What do you mean?'

'We've got to go and see the people that owe money. We've got to ask for it.'

At another time, Andrew would have laughed. 'But, darling, it isn't that simple. They are old established firms, you can't chase them like crooks! They won't do business with you again if you do.'

'Well, they won't anyway if Judge's goes bankrupt! Don't worry, I'll do the asking.'

He wrestled with this unlikely vision for a moment and then rejected it. He made as if to lie down again. 'You're being silly.'

'No, I'm not, Dad. Dad! You've got to get up, please! I

don't care if you never do anything for us again, but you've got to do this. If you don't, we'll have to go to that horrible man James Barton, we won't have any choice!'

Turning his face away from her, he said, 'Perhaps you should go there. I can't look after you.'

Rowan hit the mattress with her fists. 'I can see why Mummy left you, you don't try! I've done all this and you won't help at all. Mummy won't ever come back if the firm collapses. She might get tired of him and come back, you don't know she won't, and then what happens if Judge's has gone?'

'Will she come back, Rowan? Might she?'

Sullen, Rowan muttered, 'She might. But not if the firm goes down.'

Some vestige of interest kindled in him. Motivated by Rowan's fierce determination, he bathed, shaved, changed into business clothes. He staggered a little as they went out to the shiny new Jaguar.

Rowan said, 'I'd forgotten about the car. We can sell that.'

'It's bought on instalments,' said Andrew.

Rowan went very quiet. As they drove to the mill, she said, 'Has it been like this always? Pretending?'

Her father sighed. 'Not when I was a boy, no. We had more money than we knew what to do with ... a Rolls-Royce, silver. We had a yacht for a while but my mother, your Grandma Rose, was seasick. We went on holiday to Switzerland twice a year. Once in the summer and again to ski.'

'I was going to learn to ski,' said Rowan dismally. It seemed a long time ago, in the days of her childhood.

'When I met your mother,' went on Andrew, 'I had a lovely little sports car, British racing green and the bonnet held down with a leather strap. We went everywhere in it, driving like the wind. Diana loved it.'

Rowan gave a snort of contempt.

71

'We were so happy,' said Andrew, his voice cracking.

'Look, we're nearly here,' declared Rowan. 'Come on, Dad, let's hurry.'

Almost nothing was happening in the mill. One or two looms were going, but apart from that people stood around in groups, talking. When Andrew arrived, a flutter went through the place, a shudder of hope, of expectation. He went straight up to his office, looking at no one. 'We've got to go through the books,' said Rowan. 'You tell me who owes the money and I'll write it down.'

'There's a list somewhere,' said Andrew vaguely.

Rowan blinked at him. If there was a list, why had it not been acted upon? She didn't understand.

The secretary came hurrying into the room, a neat lady in a brown cardigan. 'Oh, Mr. Andrew! Thank goodness you're back. On behalf of everyone at Judge's I should like to say how sorry, how very sorry we were to hear about — well —'

'Hello, Frances,' said Rowan clearly. 'My father wants the list of the people that owe the firm money. We're going to go round and see them.'

Frances looked from Rowan to her father and back again. 'Is that right, Mr. Andrew?' she asked. He said nothing. He was fingering the photograph of Diana on his desk.

'Please get it, Frances,' said Rowan. 'It really is urgent.'

Frances pulled down her cardigan, because she was not the sort of woman to put up with being bossed around by children. Then, because Andrew had still said nothing, she went and got the list.

Rowan was shocked by the names, and the amounts. Thousands and thousands of pounds on which Judge's were paying interest. 'It shouldn't be allowed,' she declared. 'They ought to know what happens when they don't pay.'

'Half of them can't pay,' said Andrew wearily. 'I'll mark the ones we needn't bother with. And the really big boys 'won't pay up either, not unless we summons them.'

'Then we should do it,' said Rowan. 'They shouldn't get away with it, even if it does cost us money.'

'But then we'd lose their business,' said Andrew. 'We need them more than they need us. It's a cruel world, my darling.'

But Rowan wouldn't be put off. Finally they had a list of ten names. 'I'll write to them,' said Andrew vaguely.

'Oh no! We're going today, to see them.'

'But, darling — then they'll know we're desperate. It could finish us.'

'Daddy, if we don't go we're finished anyway. Can't you see, we have to? I'll go in, you can stay in the car if you like.'

And suddenly Andrew couldn't bear it. Her competence, her determination, completely unmanned him. He turned away, racked by dry sobs.

# Chapter Nine

In the end it was Rowan who stayed in the car while Andrew went round asking for money. The experience was a surprise to him, because he had expected contempt and ridicule, and instead received kindness. Everyone knew what had happened and few people imagined that they, let alone Andrew, would have come off best in an encounter with James Barton. They felt sorry for him, knowing how bad things were and that if they didn't pay up then they would certainly bear some of the guilt of Judge's collapse.

Back in the car, after the third successful visit, Andrew said to Rowan, 'I thought they'd think I was weak, letting the business go like this. But they're trying to help.'

'Everybody hates that man,' said Rowan.

'Do they?' said Andrew. 'They have no reason to like him, anyway. They might think it could happen to them, you know how these wool men travel. Never home, really.'

'You didn't travel much,' said Rowan. 'I mean, she'd have had an excuse then.'

Andrew held the steering wheel tightly, though he hadn't as yet started the engine. 'Perhaps I should travel more. I always feel I can't leave the mill, there's so much to go wrong. But the order book's so thin – '

'When I'm sixteen, I shall leave school and run the mill,' said Rowan. 'They you can do the travelling and get the orders.'

Andrew laughed. A warm bubble of love for his gangly daughter exploded inside him, momentarily obscuring his misery. 'Darling Rowan,' he murmured, 'you stay at school and get your exams, a mill is no place for a girl. I want you to

75

go to university. You could be a barrister, anything. The wool business is just so messy and dirty and difficult. It's on its knees in this country. When you three are grown and off our — my — hands, there won't be any need for Isaac Judge any more.'

'But what about all the jobs?' asked Rowan. 'There's always been the mill, it's a good mill, you can't let it go!'

Andrew lifted his shoulders in a weary shrug. Then he started the engine.

Diana sat in the hotel room and watched James work. She had no objection to him working if she herself had anything to do, but for almost the first time in her life she was idle. James complained if she played her violin because it affected his concentration, there were no children to supervise, no meals to cook, no telephone calls to make. Her friends had deserted her one and all, because although it might be permissible to leave one's husband, abandoning the children was something else again.

And yet she hadn't abandoned them! Just today she had gone over to the new house and instructed the decorator on a scheme for Andy's room, a striking mixture of green and ruby red. Sally was to have a little girl bedroom, all lace and pink roses, but as for Rowan — well. Would she even come? Diana had no illusions about her elder daughter, she had set her face against Barton and nothing would bring her round. She had influence over the others, too. Diana bit her lip. Perhaps Rowan ought to stay with her father, they were very close. After all, Andrew ought to have somebody.

Thinking about Andrew was unpleasant, because it meant thinking about how she had treated him. There ought to have been a way of extricating herself without hurting him so much, but in the end there hadn't been a choice. James hadn't given her one.

She glanced across at him, carrot head bent over his papers. 'James.'

'Ummmm? Yes?' He briefly glanced up.

'Are you going to do something for Judge's? You said you would.'

'I know I did. I will, when I get the opportunity.'

'That isn't what you promised. Have you heard how they're doing? Things were bad, you know, and it would be too much for the firm to go bust as well as everything else.'

James looked up properly. 'Too much for whom?'

'Andrew, of course. I was married to him for over sixteen years, James. I don't want to live with him any more but that doesn't mean I hate him! Though I imagine he hates me.'

James came across to her and knelt at the side of her chair. 'You know he doesn't. You know he loves you to distraction and always will.'

She eyed him thoughtfully. 'Will I get that from you?'

'I'm no lapdog.' He kissed the skin of her neck, but she wasn't about to respond.

'That's not what I asked.'

'Wasn't it? The trouble with poor old Andrew was that he knew he wasn't up to you, he had to buy you off with his devotion. Now, that isn't what I'm giving.' He dropped his hand to her skirt, reaching up under the hem.

Diana gasped as he touched her. 'I don't need you just to get laid, James. I can have that anywhere.'

'So you can, my darling. But don't forget I'm not Andrew, I don't let go of things. I only throw them away.'

He groped between her legs, finding the warm folds within her clothes, watching her face register slight irritation that he should arouse her when she wasn't really in the mood. 'Oh God,' she said crossly. 'I suppose we might as well, there isn't anything else to do around here.'

In one of those unexpected gestures that so excited him about her, she stood up and languidly stripped off her skirt and pants. All his sophistication died as he looked at her, naked from the waist but for stockings and suspenders, her pubic hair an auburn cloud, her legs as long and slender as any gazelle's. Lust was suddenly choking him, but as he reached out for her she pushed him back on to the floor, expertly unzipping his trousers. The initiative well and truly lost, he lay back stunned as she straddled him and then lowered herself carefully on to him.

'Oh God. Oh God,' he moaned.

'Shut up,' said Diana distantly. 'I'm sick of things always going your way.'

He was going to come, it was like an express train. Desperately he fought it, because in this he had to satisfy her. She was watching him, riding him, her eyes cool and determined, and he couldn't stop himself. The explosion of feeling engulfed him.

Diana rolled away from him. 'Thanks a lot,' she murmured.

'I'm sorry. I couldn't help it,' said James.

She wiped herself with a tissue. 'Then I think you'd better learn to help it,' she said nastily, and smiled at him with an angry glitter. Ye gods, sometimes he felt like a seal jumping through hoops. For a second, quite unexpectedly, James felt a stab of longing for his wife.

Diana called at the house when the children were home from school. This had always been her time, with Andrew at work and the day's happenings to be traded, hot off the press. As she got out of the car she could hear Andy playing the violin and she closed her eyes and stood, savouring it. Was he really better, or was it only that she hadn't heard him in weeks? Such power, at thirteen years old!

She went into the house without knocking. Sally was sitting at the kitchen table, still in rumpled school clothes, while Rowan inexpertly chopped an onion, wiping the tears from her cheeks with the back of her hand. They both looked up, startled.

'Mummy! Mummy!' Sally flung herself towards her mother, but Rowan reached out one long arm and caught her.

'Don't, Sally! Remember what she did to Daddy! And she left us!'

'Don't be so silly, Rowan,' said Diana, and came over to gather Sally into her arms. 'Have you missed me, darling? I've missed you terribly. And look at your hair, birds could nest in it. What has happened to your brush?'

'That's right, bother about the important things,' sneered Rowan.

'Oh, Mummy, it's been awful,' burst out Sally. 'We didn't have anything to eat.'

'What?' Diana stared at Sally, shocked.

'Don't be silly, Sal,' said Rowan quickly. 'She means I forgot to shop one day, that's all.'

'No, I don't,' said Sally. 'There wasn't any money. We were starving.'

'Oh my God!' Diana looked up and met Rowan's defiant gaze. 'Why didn't you tell me?'

'I'd rather we starved to death!' Rowan picked up the chopping board, onion and all and hurled it at her mother. She ran from the room, thundered up the stairs and banged into her bedroom.

Later Diana came upstairs. She knocked on the door, then went in. Rowan was lying face down on the bed.

'Darling, talk to me,' she said gently. 'We must talk.'

'No.'

'Sally's been telling me what happened. I know how you feel but you should have told me! There was no need for it. Daddy might have been better in a hospital, I could have arranged that, had you properly looked after –'

Rowan rolled over, her face red and puffy. But she was coherent. 'You'd have put him in some mental home and he'd never have got better. He's OK now really, just sort of miserable.'

'Sally says the electricity's going to be cut off.'

'Course not, I've paid the bill,' lied Rowan. She was rather worried about that actually. Dad said if they wrote

79

any more cheques the bank would bounce them, but they were due some money at the end of next week and might only be cut off for four days, if they would put it back on as soon as you asked. On the other hand it might be four weeks, and the cooker was electric and so was the heating.

'Don't you think I know when you're lying,' said Diana flatly. Rowan bit her thumbnail.

Suddenly Diana was fighting tears. 'Oh God, Rowan,' she sobbed. 'Do you have to make things so hard? I can provide for you, I *want* to provide for you, I'm not a wicked woman! James isn't a wicked man! People get divorced all the time, it isn't a crime!'

'Not officially, I don't suppose,' said Rowan thoughtfully. 'But it's worse than robbing a bank or something. I mean, if you went in with a gun and threatened to shoot people and then didn't and stole the money, well, it would only be money. Everybody would be over it in a week. But Dad won't ever get over it.'

'Oh, of course he will!' flared her mother. 'You wait, he'll have some girl in here not two years older than you, and then see how glad you are to live with him! Whereas I can give you a lovely house and James and —'

'He doesn't want us,' said Rowan. 'He won't stand us for a minute.'

'He knows you have to come to me, and anyway you haven't a choice.'

They glared at each other.

Diana went downstairs to make a cup of tea and the children, seduced by the old order, sat round and drank it. Andy was very quiet.

'Will you go?' Rowan asked him at last.

He looked from her to Diana. 'No.'

'Oh, Andy! Whyever not?'

'Because I won't live with that man. Rowan and me have done our best to keep things going and look after Dad, you and him didn't help at all.'

'But you wouldn't let me, you didn't tell me! Did she tell you I was 'phoning, did she say she wouldn't let me speak to any of you?'

Andy gulped his tea. He knew he was betraying his mother. 'I think I should stay with Rowan.'

Diana, white-faced, swung round on Sally. 'And what about you?'

Sally looked desperate. 'I don't know. Rowan!'

'I can't tell you what to do,' said Rowan. 'If you can leave Dad just because things have been tough, and go and live with that man with all his money and his evil ways –'

'Rowan, you're being ridiculous! Anybody would think he was a murderer or something,' shrieked Diana. 'Go upstairs and get your things, Sally, you at least are coming with me tonight. This house is filthy, freezing cold and you're living on baked beans and mince. You can't stay here, any of you.'

'I don't want to leave Daddy,' sobbed Sally. 'Why can't you come home and make things right again?'

'Because I can't,' said Diana grittily, putting her hands to her head. 'Just come as you are, Sally, right now. I shall be back to see about you two.'

She grabbed the child's arm and marched her out to the car. Rowan and Andy sat looking at each other.

'What's going to happen, Rowan?' asked Andy.

'I don't think she can make us go, not without going to court or something. And we can't leave here, Dad wouldn't stand it.'

'No.' Andy shivered and looked around at the disaster that was the kitchen. 'Think we can turn the heating up?'

Rowan wrinkled her nose. 'I suppose we could. After all, they're going to cut us off anyway.' She went to the thermostat and turned it up full, but somehow even when the room was at last warm it still didn't seem homely.

They didn't want to tell Andrew about Diana's visit, but

even he eventually realised Sally was missing. 'She's gone with her,' said Andy gruffly. 'Rowan and me wouldn't.'

Andrew said nothing for a moment. He looked at his two set-faced children. 'You might be happier with her, you know. She's your mother, she can take proper care of you. If you want to go I shall be quite all right, I promise you.'

'That's silly,' said Rowan. 'You'd be on your own.'

Andrew sighed. 'I went to see Mr. Blood today, at the bank. He was very impressed with you, Rowan. And − there are one or two problems. School fees for one.'

'That's all right,' said Rowan. 'We'll go to the comprehensive, won't we, Andy?'

But Andy said slowly, 'I don't mind that, but − my music lessons. We've got to afford those.'

'Yes, of course, we must,' said Andrew. 'I just don't see how at the moment. And your mother could afford them. But there is another thing.'

Rowan's heart sank. 'Mr. Blood wants us to sell the house,' she said mournfully. 'He said we might have to.'

They sat in dreadful silence, until Andy said, 'This is so awful it's like a horror film.'

'It's not really that bad,' said Andrew in an attempt at cheer. 'You two could go to your mother and I could live at the mill in one of the terraced houses. A lot cheaper, a lot more convenient and the bank balance would look a great deal healthier with the money from this place in it.'

'We'll come and live in the mill house, then,' said Rowan.

'It's a wreck,' said Andrew. 'I'll get it done up, of course, but just now − well, I'll be living in my office.'

Eventually Andy and Rowan went off to bed. The awfulness of everything drew them together as never before. They sat side by side on Rowan's bed and talked about it.

'They stab people at the comprehensive,' said Andy. 'They'd stab me if I went there, they shout when I go by in my cap.'

'I'd look after you,' said Rowan.

'I don't want to be looked after by my sister! Why can't we have that man's money and not go and live with him?'

'Because nothing's ever fair!' said Rowan. 'Something horrible ought to happen to him, to pay him out for what he's done to us. But it won't. He'll go on and on, getting more and more beastly.'

'But why did she go with him?' asked Andy, puzzled.

'Because of the diamond brooches,' said his sister. But at fifteen, she knew what it really was. When she saw James Barton she understood, as did her mother, that here was the herd leader, the stag to whom all females should submit. The attraction, felt even by Rowan who hated him, was entirely to do with power.

James was feeling rather bad-tempered. He was tired, and as he got older he noticed the below par days more and more. Living at the hotel had been bad enough, with the departing revellers late at night and clattering chambermaids early in the morning, but he had expected an improvement when they moved into Aspley Manor, especially considering what it was costing him. Sadly, things were worse. The newly installed central heating had air in it or something, and the autumn chill was striking very cold in the huge rooms and long corridors. To help things along, teams of workmen still arrived at crack of dawn. And that damned child Sally had nightmares!

He could never remember Marjorie indulging Richard as Diana did her daughter. Whatever the hour, and however many times an hour, she would respond at once to the shrieking and sit with the brat, calming her and offering to make her cocoa or something. Anyone with half an eye could see she was trying it on.

'I wish you'd stay here, Mummy, and not go to bed with him!' Sally had begged last night, so appealing in her expensive French nightgown, paid for by him. It was ridiculous and he didn't intend to tolerate it a moment longer, he would speak to Diana about it that evening.

There was a perfunctory knock on the door and Saul entered. He was wearing a cream linen suit that would not have been out of place on the Riviera. James growled, 'What the hell do you want?'

Saul studied him briefly. 'You look ill,' he commented. 'The glamorous Mrs. Judge is proving too much for you, I suppose. She won't like it if you can't get your leg over twice a night. Oysters and champagne, James, they're your only hope.'

'Mind your own damned business,' muttered James, surprisingly mildly for him.

Saul threw a folder on to the desk. 'Sales figures.'

'Up or down?'

'Up. Fantastically up, it's the new range. But, everybody wants everything yesterday, and if we don't get our fingers out the Italians will. I hate to be so businesslike but we've got to shorten lead time.'

James leaned back in his chair and stared at his half-brother. 'You're just too bloody soft, you couldn't negotiate for a sandwich. If they want what we've got to sell, you tell them to wait till we deliver.'

Saul considered. 'I know when to back off, if that's what you mean. You don't know what it's like outside, there are wolves prowling in the streets! In New York I was being followed round by the Italians. They're sending out teams. Admittedly they're so bloody snooty they alienate most Yanks but we're talking pressure here. And their stuff is good, take a look at this.' He reached into his pocket and brought out a small pack of samples, the type that salesmen distribute to customers.

James unfastened the binding and spread the materials out on the desk to study them. Even in these small pieces it was obvious that they were new designs and weaves, richly coloured and subtly blended. 'They look very expensive,' he commented.

'Nothing in it,' said Saul. 'Except lead time. If we want to hang on in there, we've got to smarten up.'

James grumbled and grunted, but production was his department and not Saul's. So, to vent his spleen, he savaged Saul about the cost of the stolen samples. 'Your expense account is an absolute fucking disaster and I want it halved!' he snarled. Then he became aware that Saul, far from listening, was looking towards the door. Diana stood there, a slightly pained expression on her face. She looked mesmeric, dressed in soft black with a little black hat on the back of her auburn hair. There was a diamond brooch on the hat and another on the dress. James almost groaned as he looked at her.

Clearing his throat, Saul said hoarsely: 'Mrs. Judge. Saul Barton, I don't think we've been introduced.'

'How do you do. I've seen your photograph in gossip columns.' She extended her gloved hand to him.

'You shouldn't believe everything you read,' murmured Saul. She smiled and then nodded coolly at James. 'James.'

'Darling.' He got up and went to her, but as he reached out to put his arms round her she moved away. 'We were having a business discussion,' he said feebly.

'So I heard. Do you always scream obscenities in the office?'

'Only at me,' said Saul. He was amazed to see James without the initiative, having assumed, as did everyone, that James had seen, grabbed and tamed the beautiful Mrs. Judge.

Diana seemed to relent. She put her hand on James's shoulder and said confidingly, 'James, dear, Rowan telephoned. She and Andy will be coming tonight and I'm in town to get some things for their rooms. We'll have a celebration meal this evening. What time will you be home?'

'Er — about seven-thirty. But they're not coming for good, are they?'

'Yes, thank God. They've been having a terrible time, I'm just so relieved.'

'But why the hell can't they live with Andrew? They said they wanted to, and quite honestly I'd rather they did.'

In clipped tones, Diana retorted, 'I daresay you would, dear, and if you hadn't reneged on your promise to help the firm, they might be there yet. Andrew has had to sell the house and move into one of the mill cottages. It needs a lot of work, and the children can't stay there. I'm sure you wouldn't wish them to.'

'Yes, I'm sure you wouldn't, James,' interposed Saul. 'I well remember how much you like children, playing with them, getting up to jokes. He locked me in the cellar once for about six hours. I was four, he was nineteen.'

'Good God,' said Diana. She didn't know if she should believe him. He spoke as if it were a joke but there was a grim undercurrent somewhere.

'Get out of here, Saul,' said James viciously.

'By all means, brother mine.'

When he had gone James went to Diana, took her in his arms and kissed her hard. She returned the kiss, almost losing her hat.

'Stop it!' she murmured. 'You're wrecking me.'

'Am I? Diana, if the children are there we won't be able to do this, you know. Send them back. I'll buy out Andrew.'

'There's nowhere to send them back to, the electricity's been cut off. Besides, it won't be as bad as you think. They'll come round, you'll like them.'

'Even Rowan?'

'Well − it's a difficult age. You must know that from your son, and he'll want to come and stay in the holidays, won't he?'

James hadn't even considered it. On reflection he supposed he might come, though he hadn't even seen Richard since the split with Marjorie. It wasn't that he hadn't wanted to − again and again he had been on the verge of arranging something, but then he thought of the conversation. How did you explain abandonment? How did you excuse lust? Not even he could tell his own son he had left home because his mother was a boring cow and useless in bed. It was a reason and a justification, but Richard wasn't old enough to understand.

'I don't want that girl screaming at me in my own house,' he said pugnaciously.

'She won't,' soothed Diana.

James was late for the celebratory meal. Diana was edgy, Sally over-excited and Andy was determinedly practising the violin in the dining- room, though they had a perfectly good music room acres away from everyone. As for Rowan, she was in her jeans and would not change, any more than she would alter her expression of sullen and fulminating resentment.

'Just don't get at him, Rowan,' her mother warned.

'Why not? Are you frightened he'll go off you?'

The violin played wildly, adding a manic background to everything that was said. Sally did a handstand, came over hard and crashed against the table. Two glasses fell over and one of them broke.

'Oh, for God's sake, Sally!' yelled Diana.

Andy played wrenching chords, one after the other, Sally burst into tears, and in the midst of it all James arrived.

Andy stopped playing. They cleared away the glass and sat down to the meal. 'Come and help carry things, Rowan, please,' said Diana.

Rowan went, absolutely silent. James turned to Andy. 'How's the playing coming?'

Andy sighed, letting it be known that this sort of inane comment was one he suffered endlessly. 'OK, thanks,' he muttered.

'Is that all you can say? I asked how it was, I expect to be told how it was,' snarled James. He would not be bullied by these children, he refused.

Andy eyed him belligerently from beneath a fringe that

87

needed cutting. 'Well,' he began, 'the concerto is coming along well though I'm having trouble with the scherzo, partly because of my age, my hands haven't developed fully. I'm disappointed in my progress this year, my mother used to teach me a lot and she's been doing other things. I was hoping to have begun some Rachmaninoff but my practice hasn't been going too well and I haven't, so I've a lot of catching up to do. And if you don't know much classical music you soon will because I play it all the time. And scales.'

'Thank you,' said James. They sat in silence until Rowan and Diana came in with the food.

Rowan had to hand round the warm plates and she did so sensibly, until she came to James's. She banged his down hard.

'Rowan!' Diana glared at her.

'It was hot,' lied Rowan. She passed round a dish of peas, managing to spill a sizeable portion into James's lap.

'Oh God! James — I'm sorry — just let them go on the carpet and I'll sweep up later,' apologised Diana.

'No, you won't,' said James. His face, always pale, had twin blotches of high colour on the cheekbones. Rowan, watching him, felt her stomach twitter with fright. What had she done? 'Get up to your room, Rowan,' rapped James. 'The rest of you eat up and shut up. This is my house and I insist on politeness and respect, even though I don't want you to like me and I don't have to like you. I will not pay for brats who think it's funny to be rude!'

'We didn't ask you to pay for us,' said Rowan tremulously. 'If you hadn't wrecked our lives you wouldn't even have to know us. You should have thought about us when you decided to — to do it with my mother. You ought to have known what we'd think of it, you filthy old bastard!'

James leaped from his place and came at her. Diana screamed 'James!', Andy dived to rescue his violin and Sally shrieked 'Rowan!' and threw herself at her sister's legs.

With Sally holding her, Rowan couldn't even run and James grabbed her long arm. But he hadn't expected to catch her and didn't know what to do now he had. Her frightened, green-eyed face was inches from his own.

'I'm warning you,' he said softly, 'I won't have you spreading your own special brand of nastiness in this house. One more outburst like that and I'll pack you back to that weak-kneed, mewling man you call a father — whether he's got a rathole for you or not.'

'Mummy, Mummy, stop him!' wailed Sally. 'He's going to kill Rowan!'

'Will you kill me?' asked Rowan shrilly. 'Because I won't be quiet. I hate you, Mr. Barton.'

Diana pulled Sally upright and then held James's shoulders. 'We'll all sit down now and eat our meal,' she said with studied calm. 'You too, Rowan. We're all upset and it will be better when we've eaten. James, I've poured you some champagne.'

James allowed himself to be somewhat mollified. 'I mean it, Rowan,' he said grimly. He had yet to learn that with Rowan he never had the last word.

'You can mean what you like, you don't own me,' she snapped. But she sat down at the table. The meal that was to have been a celebration was eaten in stony silence.

# Chapter Ten

The leaves were being blown from the trees in clouds, and the rooks shrieked as they were tossed on the wind. Aspley Manor was on an exposed rise of hill and took the worst of the weather, particularly on a day such as this, when winter was rushing in like a wild grey hag. Twigs rattled on the roof of Saul's beloved Aston Martin as he passed along the drive. He glanced anxiously up at the ancient trees that might decide to crash down to earth on any one of these days. There could be no greater contrast to James's cosy, suburban house than this.

He could see why James had bought it, though. The Manor proclaimed what he had become, it was a testament to his achievements, and the same could be said about the new woman in his life. Diana was a woman to be proud of.

Saul ran quickly up the stone steps and jangled the bell on the massive front door. The house seemed very quiet, and he had expected everyone to be at home. He rang the bell again, and after a few minutes, when his blood was congealing in his veins, Diana answered. She was very pale and there was a scratch on her forehead.

'Good God, are you all right?'

'What? Oh, my head. Yes, I'm fine. I'm sorry, we'd forgotten you were coming.'

Saul went into the hall, a magnificent entrance in panelled oak with Turkish rugs on the parquet and a marble table Diana had found in a shop in Harrogate. 'James did ask me to come,' Saul ventured. It had in fact been a command, to attend at the house as soon as he returned from his exploratory trip to South Africa. And here he was. From somewhere upstairs there was the sound of sobbing.

'Look, if it isn't convenient I can come another time,' he said. His brown eyes gazed at Diana with real concern. Some of the tension went out of her. He was younger than she yet so admiring, it restored some measure of her control. 'There's been an upset,' she explained. 'James became very angry about Andy playing the violin, and he should have been in the music room but wasn't. I yelled at James, and of course Rowan got involved, as she would, and then − well, Andy's violin has been broken. James blames Rowan, Rowan blames James, Andy's distraught and I − I think I'm going to have a total nervous breakdown.'

She laughed unhappily and Saul somehow couldn't help himself putting his hands on her shoulders. James's voice cut across them. 'What in God's name do you think you're doing, Saul? Let go of her!'

Saul did not immediately comply. James's hair was on end and his face bore the clear imprint of a handslap. 'Was that Rowan?' Saul asked, grinning.

James rasped, 'Will you let go of Diana? I know what you're like with women! Don't think you can come sniffing around while I'm out, hoping to get in her bed.'

'Oh, James! We don't have to have that sort of paranoia, do we?' Diana stepped away from Saul and put her hands to her head, and James, struggling for control, burst out, 'All right, all right. It's just − let's have a drink, God knows I need it.'

They went into the drawing-room, and the fire was dying. Cold air hung in the room as substantially as curtains. 'The bloody heating never works,' growled James. 'Why don't you ever get on to them, Diana?'

'I do, every two days,' she intoned. 'I want straight Scotch.' She went and revived the fire, throwing coal on with a vicious disregard for smoke and dust. Saul felt a deep and delighted pleasure at such disarray, it satisfied him utterly to see James backing a loser. As if sensing his thoughts, James said, 'This is as far as I'm going, Diana. I'm no martyr and I won't stand for this sort of thing, it's not doing anyone any good. Rowan goes back to her father today.'

'I thought it was Andy's violin you couldn't stand,' said Diana tightly.

'She leads him on, he's as weak as his father. Rowan's the one, an absolute bloody hellcat, she is.'

'And what about Sally? Haven't you got something awful to say about her as well?'

'She's a mewling brat. Why in God's name can't a child of nearly eleven sleep through the night?'

There was a long silence, in which they could hear the coal burning on the fire, the clink of unnecessary ice in Saul's drink. Saul said, 'Judge's is nearly broke. Andrew can't afford the children, I'm sure.'

James drained his glass and poured himself another. The booze was calming him, he was looking more like his old self. 'I'll pay him to have them,' he said with a hint of humour. 'I'll send Rowan gift-wrapped in five-pound notes. Honestly, Diana, did you ever see anything like it?'

She grinned. 'Frankly, no. Well, I suppose it's an opportunity to get Andy a decent violin at last. I'd better go and see to him, he's so shocked. It's like smashing a part of his body.'

'Poor kid,' said Saul. As Diana went out he said to James, 'Rowan must be in a state too, isn't she?'

'Save your sympathy there,' replied James wryly. 'She damn nigh knocked my teeth out. I bet you've been hoping someone would do that for years, eh, Saul?'

'I never thought it would be a girl of − how old is she now?'

'Sixteen,' said James. 'For her birthday last week I bought her a gold watch and she left it floating in the bidet in my bathroom. She makes a viper look lovable.'

It was unusual for James to talk openly to anyone. The two men sipped their drinks. Saul said, 'Are you going to get a divorce?'

'Yes,' said James violently. 'I know everyone wants to see me crawling back to Marjorie with my tail between my legs but I'm going to disappoint you. Rowan is doing her childish best to upset things and she won't get away with it. Will you take her back with you? Judge's isn't too far out of your way.'

Saul couldn't restrain himself. 'Be reasonable, James! The kid's had a terrible time, you can't treat her like some sort of parcel. You must have expected trouble. Naturally they blame you for breaking up their home, people can't be ordered to like you.'

'I don't want her to like me,' said James. 'But I will not have her spitting poison every minute of the day. Anyway, she's making Diana miserable.'

His brother eyed him ruefully. 'If that's genuine, I'm impressed. I didn't think you could care about anyone except yourself.'

He got up and went without asking out into the hall. A fair-haired girl was sitting hunched up on the stairs. Her pretty face was puffed from crying. 'Are you Sally?' he asked. 'I'm Saul.'

'Hello,' she said dismally. 'Rowan says she won't go unless he gives her five hundred pounds.'

'Well, she'll probably get it. Are you going too?'

'We'll all go if Daddy can look after us. That man's really mean.'

Saul considered. 'Yes, he is a bit of a shit. Won't you miss your mum, though?'

Sally sighed gustily. 'She likes Andy best. And I'd have Rowan, she lets me get in bed with her when I have nightmares.'

'I wouldn't think it was much fun getting into bed with James, I admit,' grinned Saul.

'Mummy likes it,' said Sally enigmatically.

Saul felt a rush of hot embarrassment. Diana appeared at the bend of the great staircase, accompanied by a tall, gangling girl carrying a suitcase. The antagonism between the girl and her mother made the air hum.

'I must ring your father and warn him to expect you,' said Diana distantly.

'I'm surprised you give him that much consideration,' retorted Rowan. The two exchanged fulminating glances before Diana stalked off to telephone.

Saul said, 'I'm going to drop you off, if that's all right. I'm Saul, James's half-brother. On the wrong side of the blanket,' he added.

'What does that mean?' demanded Rowan, fixing him with her fierce green eyes.

'My father, mine and James's mutual father, never got around to marrying my mother,' he said easily. He had given up being embarrassed about it at school, when James had made sure everyone, but everyone, knew.

'Runs in the family, I suppose,' said Rowan. 'Look, he's got to buy Andy a new violin, can you make him? If he doesn't, Andy will just die. It really is important.'

'I can't make him do a damned thing,' said Saul. All at once he very much wished that he could. The girl was so young and so strung out, the spirit within blazed with an intensity that seemed to threaten her thin body. He found her immensely touching.

James came out and Rowan at once stiffened. 'I'll buy the sodding violin as long as he doesn't play it where I can hear it.'

'I bet Mother didn't know you were a Philistine,' remarked Rowan. 'I'd watch it if I were you, she won't like it at all if you're mean to Andy.'

Since James had already realised this about Diana, he was not best pleased. 'If you'll take your brother and sister with you I'll buy him a bloody Stradivarius,' he promised wildly.

'Oh, he won't go yet,' said Rowan. 'Buy it first and then we'll see. We know all about your sort of promises.'

Saul started to laugh. James was having his nose tweaked

95

and for the first time in his life could do nothing at all about it. 'And you can stop braying like a hyena,' yelled his brother. 'Get in the car, Rowan.'

'I'm coming, too,' said Sally and got to her feet.

'That just leaves one,' said Saul. 'And it's the one that makes the most noise. I think I believe in God, James, this is your personalised Day of Judgment.'

'Go to hell!'

Saul grinned. 'I think you've got the ticket, actually. Come on, girls, we'll leave him frying.' He ushered his little flock out to the car.

Rowan sat in the worn leather front seat, restless with tension. In the back Sally gazed dreamily out of the window, lost in her world of childhood, into which adult storms and troubles were an unwelcome intrusion.

Saul said, 'You girls haven't brought much.'

'I suppose Mother will send it on,' said Rowan. Her fingers twisted together, long slim fingers with surprisingly clean nails. 'This is a nice car,' she added. 'Have you had it long?'

'Five years. I mortgaged my soul to buy it and I wouldn't sell it for anything in the world. Fortunately I'm away so much it doesn't do many miles, I spend as much time underneath as I do inside.'

'You don't look the mechanical sort,' commented Rowan, casting him a sideways glance under her long, dark lashes.

Saul realised he was making an impression. He allowed himself to admire the long legs coming together in the tightest of tight jeans, and felt ashamed of himself. The child was barely sixteen. 'Do you like cars?' he asked ingenuously.

She nodded. 'A lot more than I used to. It comes from using public transport, I never realised you can wait whole days for a bus.'

'It's not that bad, is it?'

She sighed. 'Men grow old in bus queues. And all you car drivers zoom past and never see us at all, you're too busy worrying about your overhead cams and turbo chargers.'

'I haven't got a turbo charger. The Aston would fall apart screaming if you showed her one. We think they're vulgar and unnecessary.'

'So this doesn't go very fast then?' queried Rowan and Saul conceded the point. 'Not any more, no. She's beautiful but frail and I have to cherish her.'

'Do you like cherishing things?'

Saul suppressed a grin. He was the subject of an experimental flirtation, and he wasn't in the habit of disappointing people. He changed gear, leered suggestively, and murmured, 'Very much.' To his amazement Rowan blushed scarlet, sat up rigidly straight and stared fixedly out of the window. It forced him to chuckle. 'You innocent,' he said. 'You sweet little girl.'

'I beg your pardon?'

She was looking at him out of frightened eyes, quite out of her depth. He thought of the woman he slept with at the moment, divorced from a peer and more knowledgeable in her cradle than this girl right now. 'Will your father be able to look after you?' he asked suddenly. 'I mean, if he can't you must let me know. I wouldn't want to think you were in trouble.'

It was a bad choice of words. Her cheeks flamed again. 'Thank you. We'll be quite all right,' she said stiffly.

When they reached the mill she made him stop outside the gates, saying goodbye as if giving formal thanks for a jelly and blancmange party. When he looked back in his driving mirror he saw her watching him go, a child not quite a woman, wand-thin and shivering in the cold.

The Bradford hamburger joint was run down, the seats slashed and the glass of the windows murky. It was due for revamping, when the prices would go up and the customers would change, but for the moment it catered for the lesser, poorer end of the market: the tramps, the unemployed, the flabby women with endless children and no winter shoes. Andy, Sally and Rowan sat grim-faced at a corner table.

'I still think I should leave,' said Andy. 'I mean, if Mum spends five minutes teaching me, he's yelling. They fight about it.'

'All the more reason for you to stay,' said Rowan implacably. 'They deserve to be miserable.'

'I wish we could go back to the way we were,' said Sally, but the others took no notice. It was a sentiment she frequently expressed and they had tried all sorts of answers, but still she kept on saying it.

'If they split up, there's no one to pay for my training,' said Andy.

Rowan was taken aback. This single-mindedness of her brother, often encountered, was nonetheless still shocking, like meeting a brick wall when you had thought you were stepping into the garden. 'There'd be some way,' she blustered.

'No there wouldn't. How's the house?'

'All right.'

There was no point in telling him the half of it: damp plaster they couldn't afford to hack off, ill-fitting curtains, five plugs on one dangerous socket, the strange and devious wiles of the poor that she was being forced to learn. 'I'm leaving school at the end of term,' she volunteered.

'Won't *he* pay?'

'I don't want him to. I'm going to help Dad, there's no way he's managing. He just blunders from one disaster to the next. We had a loom go up in flames last week. Dad said they shouldn't have put it out, they should have let it all burn. Except the mill isn't insured any more, the premium was huge.'

Sally sucked up the last of her watery, additive-rich milk shake. 'Dad won't let you leave school,' she commented.

Neither Rowan nor Andy said anything. They both knew that if Rowan set her mind to something, Andrew wasn't the man to stop her.

'Well, I'm not letting Beastly Barton off the hook,' said Andy. 'I'm going to make him pay for me to go to music college in London. I can board, it'll be super. If I can get through the audition.'

'You'll walk it, you know you will,' said Rowan.

He shrugged. Worms of doubt wriggled at the back of his mind. They were never far away, he could never really believe he was as good as people said. When he performed and was acclaimed he believed it, briefly, but a day, two days, later he was anxious again. He was quite serious in thinking that the audition might be beyond him. As he saw it, a year ago he would have walked it, but recently he had lost hours of practice, his mother had been distracted from his lessons, he had even found his mind wandering when always before he had possessed total concentration. He had to pass! Escape was the only, the inevitable, answer. If he was to follow that shining star, treading a cold road upward, everything else had to be left behind.

'Did you bring anything?' asked Rowan.

Andy reached into his pocket and handed over three silver teaspoons. At that moment he felt a sudden, fierce resentment of Rowan for involving him in something that took time and energy and bravado and lies. He wanted to be on his own, to be rid, finally, of his obligations. He said: 'You know you don't really have to pinch things. Mum said to ask if you needed anything, clothes and so on. She'll buy it and put in on her credit card, he'll never notice.'

'A Sindy doll!' said Sally. 'The one with the wedding dress. And Rowan needs some new jeans, hers are awful.'

'I'll buy what I need myself,' said Rowan haughtily, knowing that Andy would ensure that the jeans arrived.

It was all money. She thought about it endlessly, it even haunted her dreams. Husbanding pennies, thinking twice

99

and three times before spending a pound, always aware that James Barton had buckets of the stuff and all she had to do to gain access to it was swallow her pride. To be tempted was worse than to be deprived. How she hated this bitter, endless dependency!

# Chapter Eleven

Life had always been difficult for Andrew Judge. He was aware that other men found it easier, at times, and were therefore always optimistic about things picking up soon. In the past he too had believed that one day he would stop being anxious and would become the calm, resourceful, successful man he knew he should be. But in the end he had to face it. Some people were doomed to miss out.

Not even when he and Diana were together had he been really happy. The difficulty of sustaining life as she wished it to be had been an ever-present cloud in the sky. Looking back he realised that this had been the best part, the part he should have enjoyed most, but at the time he had worried. It was as if all along he had been anticipating what was to come.

He shivered in the chill evening air. Winter was officially at an end, as his marriage was officially over, but there was still sleet in the falling rain. The mill loomed darkly above him, and darker still were the hills around, punctuated here and there by the lights of houses. The lights of his own house gleamed behind him and there at least it was warm, but he didn't want to go inside. For the sake of the girls, who wanted to believe he was all right, he put on a pretence of contentment. Tonight, with black misery whirling behind his eyelids, he couldn't stand the strain.

So he went into the mill. He thought he might make himself a cup of tea, but the sight of Elsie's tin of condensed milk, with yellow blobs congealed on the lid, put paid to that idea. It seemed even colder inside, and because there seemed no reason to fight it he went and sat on the cold stone steps that led from his office to the weaving shed. They epitomised Judge's for him. Cold, dirty, smelling of decay, and leading down, down, down. He didn't look up, for him there was no up, it was all downhill for him and Judge's and everyone. God, how tired he was of it.

The thought came again. He had considered it four times before, and each time there had been a reason for its rejection. Because of course, something would turn up. Finally, inevitably, he realised that nothing was ever going to change, that for some reason to do with the turning of the world and the fortunes of people like James Barton, people like him had to be losers. And wasn't it typical of him that it was taking so long to decide to do something so obvious? Couldn't he at last decide something, do it and do it well?

There was a rope in the warehouse, thin nylon that would not break, for the final indignity would be to bungle it. The stone stairs had an iron handrail, and the stairwell fell straight for about twenty feet, more than enough. He tied the rope on carefully, suddenly remembering how he had been taught those same knots as a wolf-cub and had barely used them since. He felt a tremendous lightening of his spirit, as if the pressure building inside him was at last being released. This was clearly and honestly the only thing to do.

As he straddled the rail, the rope looped neatly around his neck, he wondered if he should leave a note. But what could he say that would not sound trite and obvious? That he was sorry? He had always been sorry, he was truly sorry now to be leaving the girls in that mucky little house and the mill workers out of their jobs and everybody in the lurch, but for once he was doing what was right, for him and no one else. He laughed. And slipped over the rail.

Rowan said, 'Dad said he was coming in, didn't he, Sal?'

Sally, sitting on the moth-eaten rug before the fire, her knees clasped to her chin and a copy of *Black Beauty* balanced on them, said, 'He was going to wander round a bit. He had a fit of the dismals.'

The girls exchanged glances. They were used to his moods and had their own techniques for handling them. 'He hasn't had anything to eat,' said Rowan.

Sally unravelled herself and stood up. 'I'll go and fetch him, tell him his supper's spoiling and you're upset.'

'Don't forget your coat,' said Rowan.

Sally slipped out of the little house and stood waiting for her eyes to accustom themselves to the dark. She expected to see her father in the yard, staring at things, but it was raining and he wasn't there. Sally pulled her coat round her and scampered across the puddles. High on the black face of the mill was the glimmer of a light. He was in his office.

The mill at night was scary, and usually she didn't go in, but if Dad was there, cold and miserable, she had to fetch him. She switched on the strip lights and ran through the weaving shed, calling, 'Dad! Dad! Supper's ready!' Her voice echoed in the cavernous room and she ran faster, to get to Dad and safety. The door to the stairs was half-open. She slipped through it, reaching for the light-switch she knew to be close by. Something hit her in the face. She lost her breath, found it, and in the same moment her reaching fingers switched on the light.

The scream she had been mustering turned to a ball of ice in her lungs. Her father's feet swung inches from her face, the heel of his shoe worn down on one side as it always was. There were his hands, helpless at his sides, swinging forward of the body in an unreal way. Above, suffused with dark blood, the green eyes bulging in a look of horrific surprise, was her father's face.

She reached out and touched the foot lightly. It set the whole body swinging on the end of its twenty-foot pendulum. It came at her, she couldn't get away. She thrust at it and back it swung, hitting her in the face. Somehow, when she tried to get back into the weaving shed, it wouldn't let her. It hung on to her, the legs tangling up and dragging in her way, catching on the heavy door. The scream came out, a cry of raw panic, and she was through the door and running, screaming.

She didn't stop, she couldn't stop, even when she was back in the house and Rowan was there she couldn't stop screaming. When, at last, her throat closed and she screamed no more, the noise in her head went on. It went on for years.

At the funeral, the three children stood together, wanting no-one near them. Diana came and stood apart, dressed so strikingly in black that Rowan hated her for it. She imagined her mother trying this and then that, determined to look her elegant best even at Andrew's funeral. When, at the graveside, Diana dissolved into shuddering, graceless sobs, Rowan was amazed. Sally watched with her expression of frozen fear that had stayed with her night and day. Rowan put her arm round her and it was left to Andy to go to Diana. Rooks flew from the tall, thin trees beside the gate. The hills rose up like a purple backcloth beyond them, Bradford's hills, enmeshing the city in their folds and undulations. In the graveyard the silence smothered even the cackles of the birds.

Few people came, because it was one of those messy, tragic affairs that make attendance at the funeral almost like a reproach. Life had failed Andrew, they had failed Andrew, there should have been something they could have done. As they were leaving the graveyard, Diana supported by her son, a dark-red Rolls-Royce was waiting. James stood beside it.

Normally Rowan would have savaged him, but now she was filled to the brim with tears and dared not open her mouth. Nonetheless when James saw her, he said, 'Don't think you can blame this on me. He'd have done it anyway in the end.' Rowan said nothing. She simply stared at him with wide green eyes, her face pale and anguished, almost matching that of her sister. James swallowed. Why had he said that? Surely he need not have been so brutal. Yet he could never let an enemy pass without a blow struck, and Rowan was certainly an enemy.

Diana pushed past him into the car. She said, 'Why did you bring the Rolls today? It's such bad taste.'

James sucked in air through his nose, sharply angry. Whatever it cost him in taste he had been determined to show this pauper's funeral why it was that he had won, the impossibility of letting the meek and the incompetent take the prizes. At least Diana could try to understand him instead of joining the chorus of accusation. Andy was staring.

'Are you coming?' demanded James aggressively.

'No.'

Suddenly James had to say it. 'I didn't mean this to happen, I never expected it. Perhaps I didn't know him very well. I wanted to tell you — that I'm sorry. Tell the girls for me.'

When he had gone, Andy joined the girls in the funeral car. He sighed. 'He said he's sorry. I think he is, really.'

'Like hell,' snorted Rowan. 'He can afford to be sorry now Dad's out of the way.'

'But he didn't mean it to happen. He's not all bad, Rowan, I mean he's paying for my music college and Sal's school fees and things.'

'You're going over to his side,' she accused. She had a sudden vision of how it would be. Andy, who liked anyone who helped him with his training, seduced into the Barton camp. Sally too young to fight back, drawn into the opulence and order of Barton ways. And Rowan herself, left alone, the only one truly to know what James Barton was like. She would never get over hating that man.

There was a period of limbo after the funeral, during which everything hung fire. The mill was lurching on from one payday to the next, but no one expected it to last. Rowan and

Sally remained in the mill cottage, rejecting out of hand Diana's plea that they should go to Aspley Manor. The future seemed a confused mess. They had no idea what was to happen to them but they would not go over to James before their father was even cold. Sally went like an automaton to school but Rowan simply sat at home, helpless. One evening about a week after the funeral Diana paid them a visit. Rowan let her in.

Diana said, 'You look a wreck, darling. Your hair needs cutting.'

'I'm letting it grow,' said Rowan in a sullen voice. She wasn't, particularly, but somehow she and her mother never agreed on her appearance. Diana tried to impose her style on Rowan and it did not suit, they were such totally different physical types. Next to Diana's hard-edged elegance, she always felt hugely out of proportion.

She was surprised to see that there were shadows beneath her mother's eyes and fine lines from thin nose to mouth.

'Are you all right, Sally?' asked Diana, as the younger girl remained curled up in her chair. 'I've been worried.'

'I'm all right,' said Sally in a small voice. Rowan and Diana exchanged glances. Sally was clearly not all right, but what were they to do? An experience such as hers could not be erased, however much they should like to do so.

'Go upstairs for a moment, please, darling,' said Diana, and Rowan added, 'Yes, Sally, you go on up. I'll call you.'

When she had gone, Diana said, 'I've been to the solicitor. I wanted to tell you what's in the will.'

'I didn't think there was anything to leave,' said Rowan jerkily.

'Well, there isn't really, I suppose, not if you do the sums. But the mill's still here, and this cottage and so on. He's left everything to you three, with me as guardian. Andy gets half, you and Sally a quarter each.'

Rowan found that she couldn't speak. In all her life she did not think she had ever been so sharply hurt, it was a dagger between the ribs. After all she had done, after all the love and care and effort — he preferred Andy! He had left the most to Andy.

'Why?' It was a grunt, all she could manage if she was not to howl.

'Don't be upset, darling,' said Diana with forced lightness. 'You know what these wool men are like: it's the boys who should be in the business, the girls shouldn't get their hands dirty. And of course it isn't anything really, because it will all have to be sold. There isn't any future for it.'

'But — but I was working here. I was the one involved.' Her voice shook dreadfully. She couldn't hide the pain, it wasn't possible.

'You can't have expected him to give it all to you, can you?'

'No, of course not. Just to divide it fairly. A third for each of us, that would have been fair.'

Diana sat down in one of the easy chairs, a sagging but comfortable thing they had brought from the old house. She looked very tired, Rowan realised, and rather unhappy. 'It isn't fair. I was surprised when I found out, but when I think about it I suppose I should have expected something like this from Andrew. It was what his father would have done, you see — but then you can't see, you never knew the old man well. He didn't think much of girls.'

Rowan said, 'Why couldn't Dad understand? After all, he killed himself, he wasn't run down by a bus or anything, he knew how things stood. Andy has his music, Sally's still at school, but all I've got is the mill. I mean, even if it does have to be sold, at least I wouldn't have felt so — I thought he loved me!' she burst out.

Diana went to put her arms around her, but Rowan shook her off. She addressed her daughter's bent head. 'He did love you! I think he loved you best, if the truth were known, but Andrew was never his own man. He did what other people expected — me, his father, everyone. If he'd known you'd feel like this he might just as easily have left it all to you and slighted the others. He never did have any backbone!'

'Don't talk about him like that,' sobbed Rowan.

'Why not? That's the way he was.'

Diana went into the crowded little kitchen with its second-hand units and battered fridge. A half bottle of sherry was there, probably left over from the funeral when all right-minded people had sherry in the house. She found two glasses and sloshed a measure for herself and Rowan. The girl took hers and sipped at it, making a face at the taste.

'I didn't think you were still that naive,' said Diana testily. 'It's only sherry.'

'Yes, but it's bad sherry,' retorted Rowan. 'Thick as glue.'

Diana giggled. 'Well, what are you going to do?' she demanded. 'I know better than to suggest anything, you'll only throw it in my face.'

'Only to be expected.' Rowan stared down into her glass. In the last few days she had thought about the future a lot, but in very general terms, never confronting the next hour, the next day, the next week. Time had passed and she had taken not one positive decision.

'I want to be the one to see to the firm,' she said suddenly. 'I mean, I'm the only one who knows even vaguely what's going on. I'll talk to the bank manager and sell things and so on.'

'Well, I certainly don't want to do it,' replied Diana. 'Look, I know you won't like me saying this, but James is the man to help. When I see the way he handles his business, I realise just where Andrew went wrong.'

Rowan bristled. 'He can keep his stinking nose out of it! He'd only try and get his greedy paws on anything good. I wouldn't trust him as far as I can spit.'

'Don't be so bitter, Rowan. All right, see how you get on.

But what about Sally? She looks dreadful, I thought I might take her for a holiday. Bermuda perhaps, just me and her. She'd be missing school, of course. I'd take Andy if he wasn't starting college. You don't want to come, do you, Rowan?'

'Me? No thanks. I'll have to get on here.'

The words were automatic. To Rowan's surprise she was feeling a great and delicious relief. She swallowed and felt her head spin, probably because of the sherry. She would be alone, for the first time in her life. No one to care for, no one to worry about — it was as if she was laying down a heavy burden. She tried to concentrate her thoughts, for of course there would still be the mill, which despite everything was still her responsibility. Somehow that never weighed heavy. It intrigued and demanded, and in the end gave you back just exactly what you deserved. None of the others knew how important it was, they didn't care, they didn't understand.

Rowan turned her face away from her mother. At last, at long last, she could have the mill to herself.

# Chapter Twelve

The mill began working at eight, so Rowan went into the weaving shed five minutes before the hour. To mark her changed position she was wearing the hated suit, knowing full well that it made her look gawky. Some instinct told her that if she wanted to be taken seriously it was better to look plain, but again, vanity made her tie her hair back in a big black ribbon. It didn't suit her very well because her elfin face looked peaked against such severity, but at least it was better than shaggy untidiness.

Her heart bounced a little inside her chest, not from fear but excitement. No Andrew dithering around, unsure if they should do this or that, taking everyone's opinion before his own. Now she could get on with things, without having to ask permission or justify herself, and she had nothing, so there was nothing to lose. A sudden thought came to her: would they know about the will, had they heard that it had been left to Andy? A small flame of unquenched anger licked again inside her, because of course it was not Andy's, that was merely the foible of a distraught mind. Really, she didn't think it was anyone's. The mill was the mill, and it was up to her, Rowan, to see to it.

One of the lads saw her and started to sidle away, but she called to him. 'Tony, would you go and tell everyone I want to see them, please? We'll have a meeting in the canteen, everyone's to come.'

He looked wary. 'All right, Miss Rowan. If that's what you want.'

She went through to the spinners, setting up their banks of spindles for the day in the desultory fashion of men who know they are really wasting their time. Two men nowadays where once there had been fifty. It was automation, progress and decay, all wrapped into one. They too listened to her with fatalistic apprehension, for they all expected to be out of a job by the end of the day.

She could feel eyes watching her as she went up the stairs to the canteen, deliberately choosing the route that took her past the place where Andrew had dangled. Her father hadn't frightened her, alive or dead, and his ghost would never haunt her. She thought briefly of Sally and raged inside. Who had he thought would find him?

As she went into the high, cold room that was now the canteen and in the prosperous days had housed looms and spindles, bales and bundles of wool she felt suddenly as if she wasn't in charge of herself any more. She was afraid and yet quite sure of what she must do. She could no more have turned back now than flown down the stairs and away across the frosty valley. The low buzz of conversation died away. She turned to confront them.

'I hope you can all hear me,' she croaked, her throat tight with nerves. A rumble of assent came back to her. Without a note, folding her thin hands in front of her, she began: 'I'm sure you all realise that things have been difficult with Isaac Judge for some time now, and my father's death hasn't made things any easier. For the moment, I am in charge.'

Somebody laughed, but rapidly choked it off when it wasn't taken up by others. Rowan lifted her chin. 'I assure you I'm taking it seriously,' she said clearly. 'It seems to me that we're all going to have to work very hard if we're to save anything out of the business, and we mightn't be able to save anything at all. There are just six orders to fill, and they are short runs from some of our old customers. If we got them out on time, and we never do, we'd be idle in ten days.'

'Card's gone again, miss,' said Nobby lugubriously.

'I know,' said Rowan. 'We'll send it for scrap, it takes up

112

far too much time and effort. We're also scrapping the oldest looms. And I'm going to try and sell the land at the back for building, someone might want to put an office block there.'

'We use that land for the vehicles!' someone complained.

'Oh yes, I should have mentioned that the wagons are going too,' said Rowan. 'We can't afford our own transport any more. So of course we can't keep the drivers on, or some of the weavers, and there's some others that have got to go. I've made a list.'

One of the drivers, a young and belligerent man with tattoos on both arms, pushed his way to the front. 'This isn't fair,' he said, looming with Saturday night menace.

Rowan wondered if he was going to hit her. 'It's all on the list,' she said levelly. 'This is just the people out today, there's no saying anyone will have a job soon. I'm going to see the bank manager and he might insist we close down right away, and if people want to complain and make a fuss all that will happen is they get sacked quicker.' She forced herself to look the driver in the face. 'Like now instead of tonight. Get your coat, I'm not stopping you.'

'You don't bloody care, do you?' he said. 'You just want to keep your well-feathered nest, you don't give a damn about us jobs! Living off the fat of the workers, that's you!'

Rowan bit her lip. She was scared and enraged at one and the same time. 'That's not true,' she managed. 'I'm doing my best to keep as many jobs as possible. And if I didn't care about Judge's and — and everything, I'd just let it all collapse, I don't have to bother about it!'

One of the menders, a fat woman in a wrap-over apron, shouted: 'Leave the lass alone! She's doing her best, just like her grandad!'

Rowan's head came up. 'He didn't think women ought to be in business,' she said loudly. 'You might think that as well. But there's only me that's prepared to try and make a go of the mill, so if you don't back me we've had it. Please try and understand.'

The driver, still a foot away from her, said, 'What are you going to do for transport then? One of them posh carriers?'

'I don't know,' said Rowan cautiously. 'I haven't decided what to do.'

'Well, you don't want to use them big firms,' said the driver emphatically. 'They don't give a shit about small loads, take my word for it.' He turned on his heel and went back into the throng amidst a buzz of discussion. Rowan tried to swallow but her mouth was dry.

That night she sat in the quiet little house and tried to get used to being alone. All her life she had craved solitude yet now that she had it she felt vulnerable and lonely. Still, it was good to be able to mull over the events of the day in peace, and bad to have no one to comment on them. Mr. Blood had been gloomy. If she didn't get orders she had no business; if she got them her machinery was barely up to fulfilling them; and unless some miracle happened he could see no way in which they could make it past six months. He was, however, impressed with her actions thus far. It seemed that Judge's was almost fortunate in being so far down the tube, because it made difficult decisions that much easier to carry out. There was no choosing between this or that option, it was do this or die.

Exhilaration filled her for a wild, heady moment. Such power as she had, to say to this man, 'Get your coat', to that one 'Set this up right now.' Her father had never seemed at home with it. He had been embarrassed at having it. She, on the other hand, was all too likely to let it go to her head. How hard it was to keep your eye on the point of it all, and not to become bogged down in the endless needs of the people and machines. Orders, money, profit, those were what she must pursue. But how did you get orders when you had no new sample range, when you could not even fulfil the commissions you did have? She pondered and fretted, curled up in all her long length on the frayed carpet.

There was a knock at the door. She sat on the carpet, quite

still. The knock came again, but who could it be at the mill so late at night? 'Who is it?' she called out anxiously. The front door led straight into this room, the caller was separated from her by a scant two inches of wood.

'Joe Partridge,' the voice came back. 'I wanted to talk to you.'

Her heart thundered a tattoo inside her. It was the driver she had sacked that morning. What had he come for, revenge? 'I'm — busy,' she called. 'I'll see you in the morning.'

'It's all right,' said Joe. 'I just wanted to talk about something, I won't be five minutes.'

Suppose she opened the door and he raped her? She would have no one to blame but herself. He might even stab her, although among her contemporaries rape was held to be the worse of the two, since everyone would undoubtedly say it was your own fault or think it even if it wasn't said. Of course if he did attack her he'd be arrested and surely he wasn't so stupid. He was one of the workers after all. The knock came again. She got up and opened the door.

On this chill evening the tattoos were covered with a flash motorbike jacket. Rowan noticed his face, wide with high cheekbones and a rather mashed nose. 'It's cold out here,' he said nervously, jigging from one foot to another.

'Come in,' she said, and stood aside to let him enter.

He looked wonderingly around the shabby mill cottage. Rowan was not in the least houseproud and there were books and papers spread on the thin carpet, the remains of her tea still on the table. Joe said, 'You've come down in the world.'

'I never did live in a palace,' snapped Rowan. 'Look, if you've come to ask for your job back, it isn't any use, I can't do anything.'

'Oh, I know that,' said Joe, and hovered, not saying more. Rowan folded her arms and waited until at last he was driven to speak. 'It's like this,' he began, forcing his hands into his jeans pockets. 'I want to set up doing freelance driving. I've got a van, like, and I've meant to have a go for a bit, and seeing as I'm out of a job and it's your fault —'

'Oh no it isn't!' cried Rowan.

'I didn't run Judge's into the floor,' retorted Joe.

'And neither did I!' flung back Rowan. 'Things are as they are, and blame doesn't pay bills, so stop bleating and get on with it!'

He looked nonplussed. Rowan knew that as usual she was being far too aggressive. 'I'm sorry,' she said more gently. 'You want to do carrying for Judge's, is that it?'

'Yes. Yes, miss, it is,' said Joe thankfully. 'I mean, you know I'm honest and reliable, and I'd be dead cheap. You'll have to use someone.'

'If we were doing any business, we would,' agreed Rowan. 'It's a good idea. Have you got a card or something with your address on?'

'Well, I haven't got anything proper done yet,' he admitted, drawing from his pocket a crumpled piece of paper. Rowan took it and scanned it.

'You'll have to get something printed,' she advised. 'If you want to go into it seriously. Look, I'll get in touch when we've some work, OK?'

She waited for him to go, but he stayed put. He was a couple of inches shorter than she but feet wider, the sort of man who played Rugby League and regularly spat out teeth on to muddy pitches. 'Come for a drink?' he said hopefully.

Rowan felt herself blushing. It was the first time in her life anyone had ever asked her out. Her immediate impulse was to refuse, but then, Joe had had a difficult day. So in fact had she. 'All right,' she said. 'Have you got a car?'

'Bike.'

She dusted her hands on the jeans which she wore so much more comfortably than the suit and put on her anorak. As she shut the front door, Joe said, 'Bit miserable all by yourself, isn't it?'

'I haven't had time to find out,' said Rowan, and

suddenly realised that he had asked her out because he felt sorry for her, all alone in her dismal house. But it was too late, he was handing her a helmet and stamping on the kickstart of his bike. She buckled her head into its bucket and climbed on behind him. She had never been on a bike before.

When they started she intended to hold on to the underside of her seat, but at the first corner she clutched Joe's waist and hung on. Wet road flashed past inches away, he opened the throttle and overtook two buses and a taxi. 'You all right?' he yelled back to her.

'Yes. Fine. It's fantastic!'

The wind froze her lungs when she spoke, it lashed her bare hands until they were ice. When they drew up at the pub she was gasping. It seemed impossible that something so thrilling and dangerous could be legal.

'Do you ever come off?' she asked as they went inside.

'Broke me leg once,' he said enigmatically. 'When I was young and daft.'

'What are you now?' she queried.

He paused and looked at her. 'You're too bloody clever for me. What'll you have?'

She didn't know what to choose. It had to be cheap because he was paying, but she had never bought a drink in her life and didn't know how much they cost. 'Er – beer,' she decided.

He ordered her half a pint. When he saw her determined sipping he said, 'You don't like that, do you? I can afford to pay, you know.'

Deciding on honesty, Rowan said, 'I don't know how on Judge's wages. I'd like a glass of white wine really, but I don't know how much things cost. Is it expensive?'

'Dunno, never bought it,' he confessed. 'Bit posh for me, like.'

He drank her beer as well as his own and she sipped her wine. They talked in short staccato bursts. He did indeed play Rugby League, he was good and his nose had been trodden on in a much publicised incident she had never heard of. In his own eyes Joe was a man going somewhere. Rowan wondered if she should see him like that too, because to her he looked like just a nice, energetic bloke that she wouldn't have sacked if she had known him better. 'What's your van like?' she asked.

'Beat up. But now I'm out of Judge's I'll paint it a bit. You won't be ashamed to use me, I promise. Partridge Carriers, that's me.'

Abruptly Rowan stood up and asked to be taken home. He didn't seem to mind her lack of finesse, he was equally gauche himself. In silence they mounted the bike and blasted off back to the mill, terrorising a learner driver into gibbering incompetence. Joe whizzed past contemptuously, swinging into the mill yard in one long, smooth slide.

He walked her to the door of her cottage and she turned, saying firmly, 'Thanks for the drink, Joe. I'll be in touch if there's any work.'

'Right you are.' Then, almost as an obligatory end to the evening, he put his arms round her and kissed her. Rowan felt his tongue glide between her lips, his mouth very warm and soft. Revulsion battled with pulsating waves of feeling, coursing through her body from that strange, probing tongue. She wondered if she ought to hit him. 'You got right cold from that bike,' he commented, letting her go. 'Night, miss.'

She fell through the door of the cottage. Her skin was tingling all over. So much for her superiority over Joe Partridge! He at least knew how to kiss. It was her very first, so for her it held an importance she was sure it didn't for him. He was one of those men who didn't know how to treat women if they weren't matrons or girlfriends. She sat in the old, battered armchair, drawing her knees up to her chin. It was an extraordinary end to an extraordinary day.

\* \* \*

At some time during the night, Rowan was seized with inspiration. She couldn't believe that she hadn't thought of it before. The whole thing sat in her head, perfect and organised.

Judge's would contract out all their existing orders to firms who could and would fulfil them, devoting themselves meanwhile to sorting out the mill and doing sample runs on a new range. It would mean, of course, that they would have to do a lot of running about, taking the wool they already had to be dyed, carded, then spun, woven, and finished wherever there was capacity at a fair price. Joe Partridge could do the carrying and he'd better be as cheap as he promised. The only loser would be Judge's pride, but that paid no bills. And as for the sample range ... the best thing to do would be to get a look at someone else's and copy it.

They would make no money on the orders but would lose none either, and in the meantime they would have a breathing space to plan. Machinery failure had to stop; they couldn't afford any more lost time on that stony road. Discipline had to improve as well. It was no use making a beautiful cloth if some cretin dropped it in a puddle before it was packed. People had come to accept a sloppy mill, and made no effort to keep it smart. There was no doubt but that was going to change.

She turned her mind to what seemed to her a far more difficult task. A new range and new orders. Whose samples could she copy? The only ones close at hand were Bardsey's, who of course had a lovely range of worsteds, far beyond what Judge's could produce. She had seen some pieces lying around at Aspley Manor, delicious orange and green and heavily woven black.

Of course they couldn't match that. But if – just supposing if – Judge's copied it in their own inimitable woollen way? Suppose she found out whom Bardsey's supplied and followed them round with her own, much cheaper but very similar range? You got what you paid for, in cloth as much as anything, but in an age of throwaway fashion nobody wanted things to last forever.

There was just one problem. She would have to be nice to bloody James Barton.

# Chapter Thirteen

Rowan stood in James Barton's office, her hands in front of her, her whole demeanour redolent of an interview with the headmistress. James stared at her sourly. 'Why in God's name do you look so terrible? I can't believe Diana doesn't buy you clothes, she spends a fortune.'

'I didn't come to talk about fashion,' said Rowan clearly. 'I suppose you know that Judge's is in terrible trouble?'

'I'm not lending you any money, your brother and sister are costing enough,' said James.

'It's not that.' Moving hesitantly Rowan sat herself down in front of his desk, deliberately settling her legs in a gawky schoolgirl pose. Her whole manner declared, 'This is a child, don't bother about her, she is very, very young.'

'I'm going to have to get a job,' she said meekly. 'And I wouldn't want one here because of everything, but I thought – well, I thought if I looked round, at the design side and things, I might see something I'd like to do. Something I could train for.'

'You! In design! If you've got talent in that direction, I'll eat my hat.' He leaned back in his chair, surveying Rowan as scornfully as if she were a rusty car. James, with what he believed was the complete upper hand, was enjoying himself. At last he had Miss High and Mighty where she belonged, sitting like a badly-dressed little girl asking for sweeties. He allowed himself a brief moment of gloating.

Her head drooped on that long, thin neck, like a swan with lead poisoning. It disarmed him, he felt he was being unnecessarily mean. 'But of course you can look round,' he said, covering the impulse with an offhand air. 'I'll get Saul to show you the design end, you might have some flair for it. God knows, it's hard enough to find even in the obvious places.'

Rowan looked up at him, her eyes intensely green. 'That's most awfully kind,' she said sweetly. Later James remembered that sweetness and raged at himself for an absolute gullible fool.

Saul came to the office and collected her. For a moment he couldn't relate this meek and drooping girl with the termagent he had ferried to the mill. Her hair had grown but was scraped back with an elastic band in an unbecoming ponytail.

'Good to see you again, Rowan,' he said.

'Yes. And you,' said Rowan breathily. Saul had haunted her dreams for many a night. She had imagined his hands, his deep brown eyes. Now that he was there she felt almost dizzy.

'I was so sorry about your father,' he said.

Rowan had difficulty swallowing. 'Were you? That was kind.'

'Look, I haven't time to waste on drawing-room chatter so would you please get out of here and show her the design side?' said James testily. 'She's going to look for a job in textiles, and needless to say Judge's had about as much design input as your average camel. Dullest range I ever saw.'

Saul saw Rowan stiffen and said quickly, 'Then she'll be interested in what we've got to show. Come along, Rowan.'

He hustled her out of the office. After a few strides Rowan stopped and took several deep breaths. 'If you knew what it costs me to be civil to that man!' she said fiercely.

'I think it was sensible of you to approach him, though,' said Saul.

'Do you?' He was surprised by the laughter that bubbled up into her eyes, by the look of naughty secrecy. But the next instant she had gone inside herself again.

Somehow the considered stroll round the desks of Bardsey's four designers was over more quickly than Saul was used to. He was patiently explaining what each one did and how they worked out the number of threads per centimetre and it was as if Rowan, who professed to want to know, was barely listening. She was pushing him on, looking about her, always wanting to go on to the next and the next department. He was telling her about dye selection when she said, 'Look, I know all this. Can we go and look at the samples? I want to see the range.'

There was a pause. Saul said, 'Have I been teaching my grandmother to suck eggs?'

'You have rather,' said Rowan. 'Judge's used to be a very big firm, you know. It's only recently it's been so creaky. I could have worked out pics per centimetre when I was three.'

His warm brown eyes watched her. They were the colour of syrup, heaped on the spoon. 'Are you spying?' he asked bluntly.

'Of course not.' But she didn't look him in the face. 'You don't usually show the range to people, do you? People who aren't buying.'

'No. No, we don't.'

'That's what I thought. Can I see it, please?' For a terrible moment she thought she had guessed wrongly, that he would turn on his heel and go and confront James with this latest evidence of her perfidy.

'Why do you want to see it?' he asked with surprising lack of heat.

'To see what I should be aiming at. We may never even get it out, we're in such trouble. We're so far behind the times it isn't true. Nothing we can do at Judge's will hurt Bardsey's, so it isn't wrong at all. May I see?'

Saul looked hard into her face and then away. He had an irresistible urge to help Rowan, she seemed so young and vulnerable. On the other hand, if James found out what he

123

had been doing he would most certainly be out on his ear with no job, and the one good thing about the family firm was his job. It was fun and it was lucrative, which were things James never seemed to regard as in any way essential for his younger brother. He was coming to wonder if James thought his living at all was an unnecessary indulgence.

'Please help,' said Rowan softly. 'There isn't anyone else I can ask.' Her young mouth, so pink and curved, seemed tantalisingly available. Close to she wasn't at all plain. He could admire each separate part, she could only be faulted when you observed them all together. He wondered what she thought of him, if she considered him James's creature or merely took James's view — that he was a playboy, good in a limited field. Suddenly he wanted to impress her, and more than that, to kiss her. Girls were never tall enough for him, he always got a crick in his neck kissing them, but to kiss her now he would only have to bend his head . . . .

But this girl, this child, was thinking of quite different things. He pulled himself up short. 'Just don't tell anyone I showed you,' he said gruffly.

They went together to his office. Saul pulled the heavy sample cases up on to the display table at the side and started to spread the fabrics out. 'These have sold very well recently, the orange and the black. I always display them together, they look stunning, and I show them first. Never build when selling cloth. If you bore them at the start you've had it. Show your best right off and don't let them tell you it's bad. If they say it's bad, tell them they're out of date and go on to something else. They might come back to it.' He couldn't resist resting his hand on her knee as he spoke. She seemed barely to be aware of it.

'Can you tell me who you sell to? I mean, how do you get orders?'

With an effort of will he took his hand away. It would have been so easy to slide it up towards her crotch. He imagined her squeal, her falling back, his fingers miraculously finding her tight, wet opening. He said hoarsely, 'I've a list of people I visit. There'll be one at Judge's somewhere, but I don't think your father was trying very hard the last couple of years. Too many refusals get you down, there's no escaping it. You add to the list all the time, you have to have ears like a bat, listening all the time for names. Overseas you use the trade missions and the embassies, agents and people. There's a track, you just have to find it. Some people won't see you, so you try and get an introduction through a back door, someone who knows someone, or use a backhander if you're anywhere in the Middle East. It helps to speak the language.'

'What do you speak?' asked Rowan, who had just scraped French 'O' level.

'French, Spanish, Italian, some Japanese, better Arabic,' said Saul. 'I've an ear for it.'

'Good heavens!' Rowan was impressed.

Saul squashed her against the table as he reached for some more samples, plain white this time in an interesting weave. The heat of his leg could be felt through his trousers. He embarrassed her. As she leant over the table his hand rested on her back, in a brotherly fashion.

Rowan said shrilly, 'Who have you sold the orange to? And the black?'

He rattled off some names that meant nothing to her, and the one or two that she recognised were far too large for her to tackle — yet. She looked down at the floor and nibbled her lip, a habit her mother hated.

Saul paused in his listing. 'What's the matter?' he asked gently.

'Could you write down some names for me?' she asked. 'I don't want it to be your customers, though of course we wouldn't ever compete with you. I wouldn't bring you into it at all. Just some people I could visit. I know Dad had the firms he usually went to, but if they'd been going places they wouldn't have bought from us. Our cloth is really dreary, you know. By the way, are you getting a lot of burr in the wool?'

Saul blinked. 'I don't know — I suppose our combing plant could tell you.' He almost felt like lying, it was so satisfying to please her.

Rowan sighed. 'Oh yes, I forgot. You don't have anything to do with it until it's all nice and neat.'

Saul picked up the scorn in her voice. 'We don't have such an easy life, you know. And actually James is buying the comber's.'

'Whatever for?'

'Power, I should think. Bardsey Combers will be supplying quite a few of the competition, we shall know exactly what they're doing and how much they're paying in material cost. And he's getting it cheap, they're making a loss right now.'

'He's so bloody conceited,' she said bitterly. 'James Barton's magic touch.'

'What about Rowan Judge's?' teased Saul. But she didn't take him up on it.

Instead she edged back towards the subject that really interested her. 'It is difficult to know which firms really deserve your attention,' she ventured. 'After all, I might go to a firm that you know is making a loss and I'd get an order, but they wouldn't ever pay. That would be dreadful, wouldn't it?'

'Terrible,' said Saul. 'You're very persistent, aren't you?'

She drooped again. 'It occupies my mind,' she said sadly.

Half an hour later Rowan emerged from Bardsey's with the vital list of names folded into a small square in her pocket. Saul had been amazingly easy to lead. They began with firms he knew about, progressed to firms he visited, and finally he told her which ones had bought what. She was in a hurry now, to get home and make notes next to each name before she forgot it.

A voice interrupted her frenzied mental recital of facts

and figures. 'Hey! Miss!' A battered transit van drew up next to her. Inscribed in professional letters on the side were the words 'Partridge Carriers'.

Rowan hurried across and pulled open the passenger door. 'Take me back, Joe. And shut up, I've got to write things down.' She climbed up and pulled out her list, sitting crouched over it, scribbling with a pencil.

'Is that important?' asked Joe.

'Shut up!'

Obediently he drove in silence back to the mill. The road twisted and turned, at one point winding round the steep corner of a hill to reveal half the city spread breathtakingly below. The ground seemed to fall away in front of them so that they might almost have been about to plunge into the black ribbons of terraced houses, or down amongst the pin-dot cows in luminous green fields. Against the blackened stone, all the greens seemed to gain something.

'Grand view,' said Joe conversationally. Rowan barely grunted. Even when they were in the yard she did not look up but scribbled on, furiously. Joe sat beside her, stolidly silent, until at last she let out a sigh. 'Got it. Thank goodness I saw you, I'd have forgotten half before I had a chance to write it down. Right, how's the work going?'

'That's what I wanted to tell you. I don't think they're busting a gut at the spinner's. Took the wool there this morning, they didn't look at it. Just told me to sling it in a corner and they'd see to it when they had time. Place is groaning with big lots from posh firms, they won't do us on time.'

Rowan added her groans to those of the spinners. 'OK, go and get it back,' she said. 'I'll 'phone and tell them we didn't like their attitude. I'll put the men on tonight and they can spin it here.'

'That'll cost a bit,' said Joe. 'Double time, I shouldn't wonder.'

She shrugged. 'I just feel we shouldn't ever deliver late,

whatever it costs us. Never, never, never. So they can do the spinning when everyone else has gone home. People won't get in the way then, moving things.'

'What things?'

For answer Rowan slid her list carefully into her pocket and got out of the van. She marched into the mill, Joe following at her heels.

They confronted a scene of turmoil. The offending card was being dismantled, bit by bit, and the dust of generations was covering everything. Several looms were also on the way out and others were being stripped down to bare metal. Industrial vacuum cleaners were roaring importantly and when they ceased there was a clatter from the roof, where men crawled about nailing on felt and repairing skylights.

'This'll cost a bit,' said Joe, and it struck a raw nerve.

'Don't keep saying that!' exploded Rowan. 'Look, the house brought in quite a lot and all this machinery's being sold off to Africa and places, the agent said. It won't be easy doing the spinning because everything's being cleaned and mended, but it's got to be done.'

'If you say so, miss,' said Joe doubtfully. 'Just so long as I get paid.'

'Just so long as you do the job right,' retorted Rowan. 'I can't stand here gossiping. You go and get the wool, at standard rate, and I'll ring up and square it with them.'

When Rowan was older she cringed to think of herself at almost seventeen. She barged in where angels feared to tread, ringing people up and telling them she hated them, confronting aged workers to say that if they didn't stop bleating about the old days and do things her way, then they were out. It seemed to her quite sensible to ask to speak to the managing director of the spinning company and to tell him straight that they were a lousy firm, inefficient, probably without morals, and that her wool was being removed before it became corrupted.

The net result was an explosion in the spinning firm, the

128

Judge wool was found and dragged from under the very nose of Joe Partridge, and went through the mill at breakneck speed. The managing director accompanied it on its travels like an outrider at a royal engagement; he was not going to be told by a slip of a girl that they couldn't do their job. Major customers had their orders set aside without apology while the little parcel of wool went through. Thirty-six hours later it was back, spun, at Judge's, and before thirty-seven hours had elapsed it was off again to a commission weaver.

Rowan judged that they could be allowed all of five days to produce the woven cloth, and again she rang the company to speak to the managing director and explain that if this couldn't be done she didn't want excuses but hard cash. It was the courage of seventeen that drove her, the inexperience that made her see all things in black and white. At sixteen she would have lacked the confidence, at eighteen she knew too much. But at seventeen she had the fire and the morals of an avenging fury.

But then a problem cropped up which caused her much anxiety. It was her appearance. If it was all right, and advantageous, to look dowdy in some circumstances, it was all wrong and self-defeating to look anything other than glamorous when trying to sell things. What was she going to wear? The problem seemed to her so important that she took time off work and tramped the streets trying on clothes in shop after shop. She even went to Harrogate, which she couldn't afford, to see what was there, because Diana often shopped in Harrogate, especially since James had put his coffers at her disposal. How Rowan wished her mother was at hand to be tapped for one expensive present.

When at last she admitted defeat she was so depressed she spent an uncharacteristic pound on a coffee and a cream cake in Betty's. It seemed a trivial sum when set against the hundreds it would need to kit her out in executive style. She did not dare look cheap, and yet cheap was all she could afford, with her arms protruding from nylon sleeves and skirts that seated in a week. On the train back to Bradford she even considered making something herself, although her only construction thus far in life had been a cookery apron that had caused the domestic science teacher to write on her report: 'Rowan lacks that dexterity so necessary to successful needlework. She would be advised to practise sewing on buttons.' Rowan had not sewn on buttons and was presumably as hamfisted as ever.

Wandering hopelessly back through Bradford's streets to catch the bus, she passed her father's old tailor's. As a little girl she had gone with him to have suits fitted, or a camel coat made. The window was dark and filled with dark material, but inside there was a light. They had talked and laughed, her father and his tailor, exchanging gossip and still having time for her. She pushed open the door and went in.

The tailor was sitting at his worn desk, surrounded by bolts of cloth, half-made suits on a rail beside him. The room was shabby but, as Rowan knew well, in Bradford that was no guide to prosperity. 'Hello, Mr. Suzman,' she said shyly.

He looked up, taking off his half-moon glasses. 'Good heavens. Is it — Rowan Judge? My dear, I was so sorry about your father.'

'I didn't think you'd remember me.' She stood shyly twisting her hands. He waved at her. 'You always were a very tall child, with such wonderful green eyes, and you are still much the same. How can I help?'

Now that it came to it she was embarrassed. He brought out a chair, its collapsing bottom covered by a worn cushion, and patted it invitingly. 'Is there something I can do for you, my dear? Be quick, my wife will be waiting with my dinner. I can't tell her I've been chatting to a pretty girl!'

She smiled obediently. 'It's just — I need some clothes, Mr. Suzman. I know you're a man's tailor, but I'm so tall I can't get anything to fit. And — I'm in the firm now. We're not doing very well. I wanted a dress so I could go out selling, and I can't afford the sort of thing I need.'

The expected amused rejection did not come. 'What sort of dress, my dear?'

'Something in wool. Plum-coloured wool, very plain. Everybody always thinks that sort of thing is expensive.'

'But isn't that a little old for you, Rowan? You must be — well, no more than seventeen.'

'No, I'm not. I need to look older, Mr. Suzman, ten years older at least.'

He laughed. 'Impossible! I can give you five at most, I think. Of course I shall make for you, I make for all my four daughters! I have no such wool now but if you come back in two days, I shall measure you and we will begin. All right, my dear?'

She blinked at him. 'I was so sure you'd say no.'

He tapped her nose with a long finger. 'As I say, you are still very young. We will make you a beautiful lady!'

Two days went by and Rowan presented herself to be measured. She had feared it might be embarrassing, but Mr. Suzman's impersonal flicking of a tape across her shoulders and down her back was entirely functional. He wrinkled his nose at her bust measurement. 'We shall give you curves you do not have. Eat more and worry less, that's my advice.'

'I eat like a horse,' she complained, and he retorted, 'If you were a horse of mine, I would shoot you! Entirely out of kindness, you understand.'

They laughed. 'Can I see the material?' asked Rowan diffidently.

He was already engrossed in jotting down figures. 'At your fitting. A week, all right?'

'Yes — yes, thank you.'

She was out in the street, task completed, and half an hour to wait for a bus. Impatient as always, she started to walk home and after a few minutes Joe Partridge's van passed her, travelling the same way. She waved frantically and shouted. He pulled up a hundred yards ahead.

'Hello, Ro. Missed the bus, did you?'

'Yes. It takes me ages to get around, I just wish I could drive.'

He sniffed and looked thoughtful, barely waiting until she had scrambled up before driving off. 'Teach you, if you like,' he said diffidently. 'I mean, you could get yourself an old banger on the firm, couldn't you? Teach you in that.'

For a second Rowan thought her heart would explode with gratitude. To drive was her truest wish, she longed to be able to do it. No more trains and buses, no more hanging around waiting on others' convenience. She had thought her whole selling career would have to be conducted by expensive and hard to come by taxis.

'I shall never forget this, Joe,' she said fervently. 'It's the most wonderful thing anybody could ever do for me.'

He sniffed. 'Righto then. Glad you're pleased. I'll look out for something cheap, OK?'

They bumped along the road, quite silent. Rowan felt immensely and precariously happy.

The dress, her tailored dress, was all that she had requested and more. She had asked for plum, and instead she had deep, purplish burgundy. Against the wool her hair gleamed like a raven's wing, her green eyes sparkled and her skin came to life. Somehow Mr. Suzman had created bust and hip where there was very little of the real thing, darting in to her narrow waist and lightly padding the shoulders. The length was an inch above the knee, which seemed chic and elegant.

'At least twenty-five,' said Mr. Suzman. Rowan was beyond speech, she merely nodded, helplessly staring at her reflection in his pock-marked mirror. 'And I said to myself,' he went on, 'what is the use of being a tailor if you cannot make jackets? So, I make you a jacket.' A conjuror's flourish and he brought out the jacket, the same plum wool, braided in black.

'It's just perfect,' gasped Rowan. For the first time in her life she was wearing clothes that fitted. She had never seen herself look like this; to stare into a mirror and see a svelte and elegant lady cast her into confusion. All her preconceived notions of who she was and how she should behave seemed cast in the dust, because this lady was calm and well-spoken, she almost certainly played the piano and had spent a lifetime practising sewing on buttons. She wasn't Rowan at all.

Mr. Suzman let out a cry and ripped the sleeve off the jacket. Rowan gaped at him, helpless. 'What are you doing? You're ruining it.'

'I ruin my reputation if I let you walk the streets in that. Such a crease − my girls are fools! Take the dress, come back in a week for the jacket. It is a disaster, useless! My career's at an end, I am losing my touch!'

'I'm sure you're not,' she said hastily, and saw that he was laughing at her. 'I'm sorry, my dear, I'm teasing you. You are so serious! Life is a game of snakes and ladders, up so high and down again, bump! But there is a crease in the jacket, so off with you, off with you.'

Her dignity was a little damaged. 'I must pay you for the dress,' she said stiffly. 'It's so lovely, it must cost a lot. How much?'

He intended to wave it away, but he saw that would not amuse her. The girl bristled with pride. 'I had the material anyway, it isn't the best quality. Twenty-five pounds for dress and jacket.'

'My father used to pay far more for a suit!'

'Well, yes, a man's suit is much more work. This is a great deal easier.'

She beamed because she had been in agony about the cost from the moment she tried on the dress. The notes were pulled at once from her bag and thrust in handfuls at Mr. Suzman. 'I want to see you again,' he said as she left. 'Next time, we shall make something a little more amusing. Time enough to look twenty-five when you last saw fifty!'

# Chapter Fourteen

James was rather bored. With Diana away there seemed to be
endless hours in which to work, and when all the work was
done, as it was this evening, there was nothing to do. Another
two weeks before she came home, and filled the house with her
own sharp mixture of wit and sex and determination. The latter
had surprised him. When she set her mind to something, not
he nor anyone else could divert her from it. James didn't mind
on anyone else's behalf but he did where he was concerned. He
preferred to think that he held sway over her.

He went to the window and looked out into the dull, dank
evening. God, but this house was a barn when you were the
only one in it. If Diana was here what would they do? Have a
drink, go to the theatre, go to bed and screw each other
stupid. He felt a shudder of desire, and anger at Diana for
swanning off and leaving him like this. What was he supposed to do with her gone? Find a prostitute or something?

He toyed with the idea, making a fantasy of what he would
do if he was with a prostitute. Of course he would never go,
you'd catch something unless you used one of those rubber
johnnies — which he could do. After all, every man ought to
find out what was on offer just once in his life. His youth had
been spent working hard and being scared of women, he
must have missed more opportunities than anyone alive! The
years had flicked past faster than he would have believed. If
he didn't enjoy himself now, there wasn't going to be much
chance later. Everybody paid for it at some time or another.

He laughed, and felt himself good and hard in his pants, as
if he was a boy again. What did you do, just drive up to a girl,
get her in the car and screw her? He had a vision of some

whore, probably chewing gum, chatting boredly about the weather while he shoved at her. Somehow the thought of it excited him further. Before he knew it he was picking up his keys and going out to the Mercedes.

But he was only going to look. He would drive along Lumb Lane and see how grotty they were and he'd come back and have a whisky and go to bed. He might even tease Diana by saying he'd gone to one, that should frighten her. He'd tell her after they'd made love, and tease her all the way to the special clinic. There was more than one way to revenge yourself on someone you thought deserved it.

The car was warm and comfortable, a haven in which he felt totally in charge and at home. An all night chemist was open, and he stopped, hopped out and bought a packet of sheaths from the girl assistant. She handed them over without a blink, which in some way made him think that he was being left behind, that everyone else, at least all her customers and perhaps the girl herself, really was indulging in some wild sexual free for all. Why should he be the one to miss it? He'd wasted all those years being faithful to Marjorie and she, the cow, had waved goodbye to him with barely a tear shed. She didn't give a damn about him when it came down to it, all she was interested in was her knitting and her garden. What price fidelity then? And what was Diana doing all these weeks in Bermuda?

The turret and portcullis gates of the park showed up as white ghosts, monument to extravagant days when these suburbs had been stuffed with wool barons and their money. As he drove further into the city he began to weave his way through streets of narrow terraces, gathered round the mills like the tracks of snails.

The long nose of the car swung smoothly into Lumb Lane. By day it was seedy and unappetising, dotted with unwholesome Asian takeaway cafés with barred windows. At night it took on a different air, of seductive shadows and dim lights. Groups of girls stood around, and some were on their own, standing on the kerb as if waiting to cross the road. They all had the same stance, weight on the back leg, the other thrust out in front. They all wore very short skirts, some wore stockings.

One or two were revolting, fat old women in tight tops, but others were very young. They watched the cars drive slowly on, and they waited, and waited. The car in front of James drew in to the side of the road. A girl with dirty blonde hair leaned down, spoke for a few seconds, then got in. 'Damn,' thought James. 'She was OK, that one.'

He passed a short one with a plump, full figure. As he drew near she stuck out her breasts and threw her head back, pouting at him in a kiss. Without intending to stop, James put his foot on the brake. He pressed the button for the electric window. 'How much?'

She leaned in, businesslike. 'Ten quid to you. Ought to be twice as much, flash car like this.'

'Don't be greedy. OK then, get in.'

She opened the door and got into the passenger seat. She turned and smiled at him, pulling down the neck of her tight nylon top so he could see her cleavage. 'Drive up the end here and turn left,' she instructed. 'There's a place round the back.' Following her instructions they came to a long blank wall, that bordered a canal or an institution or something. The street light had been broken and it was in darkness. One other car was parked there.

The girl wriggled and pulled her skirt up round her waist. She wore stockings and suspenders but no knickers. Her pubic hair was a sparse brown matt and she smelled all right, not of soap but of animal sweat and, faintly, semen. 'Give us the money,' she said matter-of-factly. He pulled out ten pounds and gave it to her.

'How many have you had today?' he asked.

'You're the first,' she lied glibly. 'I've only been doing it two weeks.'

'Don't give me that! I don't mind how long you've been

doing it. But how many today?'

'You a journalist or does it turn you on?'

'Turns me on,' admitted James. And it did, he was as hard now as he would ever be.

'Then you'll be the tenth,' she said. 'And if you take much longer you'll have to pay double, I can't waste all night. Does this seat tip back? I get terrible backache sometimes.'

James touched the switch that put the seat back. Then, as the girl lay and watched him, he unzipped his trousers and tried to fit a condom on to his erection. 'Another fiver and I'll do it for you,' she offered. He gave her five pounds. Her hands on him were warm and slightly sticky.

When he got on top of her, he didn't immediately go inside. 'For fifteen quid I ought to see your tits,' he demanded. Sighing, she pulled them free, her top and her bra cutting into the underside, forcing them up like an obscene cartoon. He grabbed them hard and she said, 'Oh Christ, steady on!' But when he touched her nipples she laughed and said, 'Go on, give 'em a lick,' like a nanny letting her charge have an ice lolly. He thought how many other men had licked her, and he hung on at the entrance to her body, prolonging the moment. But she had her living to earn. Lifting her hips she expertly slotted herself on to his penis, rocking herself up and down on him.

'I like your arse,' she said chattily, holding it in a vicelike grip. She closed her legs a little and bore down on him. All his experience in marriage was that women tried to prolong it, but she wanted him out as fast as possible. Her hand slipped between them and gripped him, he couldn't help but come!

As he tried to subside on her, panting, she slid away from him and neatly removed the condom, flinging it out on to the road. 'Right, smashing,' she said. 'Drive me back, will you, love?' Head spinning, he took a few deep breaths but she was tutting impatiently. He started the engine and drove carefully back the way they had come. Was that all of it, all there was to it? He felt pleased and vaguely disappointed. As she made to

138

get out, he said, 'Look, suppose I wanted two of you together?'

She pushed her shoulder up, easing her bra. 'Right little raver you are. Tomorrow OK? I'll get my friend Marje, she's got a place. Be here about ten. Cost a lot though, sixty quid.'

It thrilled him to think that a prostitute had the same name as his ex-wife.

'I'll give you more if you give me a good time,' he said, grinning.

'We are going up in the world,' said the girl, infinitely bored by it all.

Once home, James scrubbed himself to get rid of any taint then slid between cool sheets. It had on the whole been better than expected: no false enthusiasm, no criticism, just a businesslike opening of the legs. If that was professionalism, he was all for it.

A thought occurred to him. If he had discovered prostitutes earlier, would he ever have gone with Diana? For once he felt uncomfortable. She should never have left him for so long, that was all it was. He pictured her at his side, so beautiful and stylish, encapsulating talent and femininity. But prostitutes came with no strings attached, while Diana, whom he had expected to leave everything for him, was encumbered with those blasted kids. It was just the kids that got in the way. When the two of them were alone they wanted for nothing.


'Here, have you seen this?' demanded James, barging into Saul's office, the *Yorkshire Post* waving in his hand.

'What?' asked Saul, squinting painfully. He had been at a party last night and could remember very little after dancing the conga in and out of some house or other. Had the house-owner even been at the party? He seemed to remember some rather annoyed onlookers.

'This bloody article! Listen: "Isaac Judge Ltd., thought by many to be on the verge of collapse following the tragic death of chief executive Andrew Judge, has landed a huge new order. L. G. Knowles & Son, who supply many of the top retail names in the High Street, has asked Judge's to provide woollens for several of their ranges. 'We were most impressed by the firm's approach and presentation,' said Mr. Samuel Knowles yesterday. 'They knew just what we wanted and were prepared to provide it at a most competitive price. We are all very pleased.' This order should ensure there are no further sackings at Judge's, where fifty jobs went only last month." '

Saul looked down at his blotter. God Almighty, she'd got Knowles. It had taken him nearly a year to crack that particular nut. But, of course, Rowan had a head start. 'Aren't you pleased?' he asked. 'She's doing OK.'

'And what in all Hades was she doing here bleating about wanting a job? My God, if Diana was here I'd make her bust that firm! One minute the girl's in here sniffing about, the next she's got in with one of our best customers! I mean, they'll fall flat on their faces because Judge's hasn't got the machines to cope with much, but she got it. How?'

'I've really got no idea,' said Saul patiently.

'What did she offer you? A quick screw down a back alley?'

Saul was on his feet and at him. James wasn't expecting it, he had flung the insult automatically. Saul's first blow caught him in the chest, his second grazed the point of his jaw. He stumbled back against a cabinet, ducking sideways out of some animal survival instinct. Saul was blazing mad, murderous!

'Mr. Saul! Mr. James!' Saul's secretary stood frozen in the doorway, clutching a tray of coffee. As another fist hit him in the ribs James dived to the floor at her side. Heroically the secretary stood her ground, holding her tray and wailing, 'Please, Mr. Saul! Do please stop!'

Saul fell back. He swallowed down thick, gluey saliva. His loss of control shocked him. He had often thought about hitting James but had never before been driven to it. Somehow James had put his finger right on the sensitive spot.